SHADOWS IN THE STONE

SHADOWS IN THE STARS
BOOK 3

T.W.M. ASHFORD

Copyright © 2025 by T.W.M. Ashford
All rights reserved.

No part of this book may be reproduced in any form or by any electronic or mechanical means, including information storage and retrieval systems, without written permission from the author, except for the use of brief quotations in a book review.

Any characters in this publication are fictitious and any resemblance to real persons, living or dead, is purely coincidental.

Cover design by Tom Ashford

DARK STAR PANORAMA

Dark Star Panorama is the shared universe of sci-fi stories in which *Shadows in the Stars* takes place. Other series include *Final Dawn, Kapamentis Crime* and *War for New Terra*.

To hear about new releases and receive exclusive free content, sign up for T.W.M. Ashford's mailing list at the website below.

www.twmashford.com

BOOKS IN THE "DARK STAR PANORAMA" UNIVERSE

Final Dawn Series

- The Final Dawn
- Thief of Stars
- A Dark Horizon
- The New World
- The Tin Soldiers
- Ghost of the Father
- The Stellar Abyss
- The Edge of Night
- The Fatal Dark

War for New Terra Series

- Sigma
- Iron Nest
- Royal Blood

Shadows in the Stars Series

- Shadows in the Stars
- Shadows in the Snow
- Shadows in the Stone
- Shadows in the Sands

Kapamentis Crime Series

- A Cut Below
- Cut to the Bone

- Cut and Shut
- The Final Cut

Standalone Novels

- Saturnalia

SELECT NON-DSP TITLES

- Checking Out (Box Set)
- Blackwater (Box Set)
- The Portrait Lingers Like a Whisper
- Gerald Oddman

SHADOWS IN THE STONE

CHAPTER ONE

Sheni pelted through the cobbled streets of Victorium as the city's grand clocktower ticked down to midnight. Pale glow-orbs burned through the mist like eerie moons. The stone walls were rain-slick and coated in moss. Dark towers and iron gates loomed at every turn.

Things hadn't gone exactly to plan.

It was supposed to be an easy job. That's how it had been sold to them, at any rate. Victorium was a small city-moon of cold slate, brass steam engines, and pea soup fogs. A guard captain down by the port by the name of Rago Porchard had a reputation for confiscating any cargo that caught his eye, and one such confiscated item just happened to be the brooch of a long-dead Luethian aristocrat – a trinket that would fetch a pretty nice price on the black market.

Rago had 'liberated' it from a spacer who had presumably stolen it off someone else – someone who might pay good money to have it back. The way Sheni saw it, they were doing the galaxy a service by taking it out of corrupt hands. And how much more stolen could the brooch get, anyway?

Gecki had slithered in through an open window on the second storey and unlocked the guardhouse's side entrance from inside. From there it had been a quick sneak down to the hold in the cellar where the brooch was stashed. They'd snatched the velvety box that contained it off the shelf without setting off any alarms. So far, so good. But then Sheni had got cocky and thrown open the wrong door, and they'd found themselves face to face not with a deserted cobblestone alleyway as planned but a whole garrison of rather confused guards.

And it turned out they weren't stealing from any old backwater thugs after all. Victorium was under Ministerial jurisdiction, which meant it was patrolled by well-armed executor squads. Ones that, corrupt or not, took a rather dim view of thieves breaking into their guardhouse in the dead of night.

So now, thanks to that teeny-tiny oversight, they were on the run with the full weight of the Ministerium on their arses.

Well, maybe not the full weight. A small dumbbell's worth of Ministerium, emphasis on the dumb. But that was still more than enough officers to toss his crew down some dingy black-site hole until they were too old and tired to try and climb back out.

Sheni scampered through a narrow crack separating one time-worn boarding house from another, his hands slapping against the cold, moist brickwork, his fingers scratching at the crumbling grey mortar. The skin on the back of his neck was stretched taut with goosebumps, and sweat glued his shirt to his back. He could hear the thunderous boots of angry Ministry officers stomping down the streets behind him.

He emerged into a barren back yard filled with old

crates and empty tin tubs and barged his way through a rusty cast-iron gate adorned with a crown of six-inch spikes. A seven-foot reptilian barrelled into him from the poorly lit through-lane running perpendicular to the yard.

Gecki yanked him out of the puddles and shoved him in the direction of their ship.

"Any sign of Iskar?" he asked, rubbing his bruised ribs.

"Not since we left the guardhouse." Gecki sniffed at the cool, misty air. "Maybe the officers got him."

"Don't be so heartless, Gecki. We can't just leave him behind."

"Hey. He ain't crew. If he gets caught, he's on his own."

Victorium wasn't like Kapamentis. Only those with dark intentions and careers of ill repute prowled the streets at night. Nightgown-clad citizens leaned out from second and third storey windows at the commotion. Many quickly slammed their shutters when they saw Sheni and Gecki coming. A bell began to chime a few streets away, alerting more guards to their presence. Sheni felt his lungs start to burn.

"How much further?" he gasped.

"Far enough that I don't fancy your chances," Gecki snarled irritably. "Didn't I tell you to get in shape in case we have to run?"

"Yeah," he spluttered. "And *I* told *you* that if we have to run, something's gone terribly wrong!"

A plasma slug screeched down the street and exploded against the century-old stone wall beside them in a bloom of amber.

"And when has anything gone terribly *right* for us?" Gecki rasped.

As they passed under a gated archway, a shadowy figure hopped down from the slate roof of a nearby shed. Gecki raised the claws of her right hand ready to slash downward and spill the assailant's intestines into the overflowing gutter, then balled her hand into a fist instead.

It was only Iskar Barabba, the third member of their haphazard heist. A regular at the Corpse & Casket space station, he'd been the one to approach Sheni and Gecki with the intel on Rago Porchard and the confiscated jewellery. His hood fell back to reveal lime green eyes that stood out against the tufts of blue feathers sprouting from his temples and running like a mohawk down the centre of his head.

"The guards are closing in," he said, holding out his hand as he jogged alongside them. "Give me the brooch."

"No way." Gecki clutched the package to her chest. "My ship, my score."

"How is it your score? I'm the one who came up with the idea."

"And look where it's got us. You want your cut? Then shut up and lead those executors away from the ship. None of us get paid until we get this thing off-world, anyway."

Iskar grumbled and then vanished down a crooked side alley.

"You're not planning on double-crossing him, are you?" Sheni wheezed. "I know he's a bit of a twerp, but…"

"Nah, course not." Gecki looked down her short snout at him. "Pirate code, or whatever. Besides, if we ditch him, who'll ever want to work with us?"

"After this shambles of a job, you sure that's a bad thing?"

Gecki grabbed Sheni and pulled him into a columned doorway the light from the glow-orbs lining the street couldn't reach. Her face inches from his in the darkness, she raised a claw to her scaly lips.

Heavy footsteps coming their way. Sheni gulped and tried to keep his knees from knocking together. If the Ministry caught him robbing from them, even on a hinterland planet in the outer systems like this, they'd lock him up in some asteroid-mining penitentiary for sure…

"They had to come this way," somebody grunted in a thick, weighty accent. Rago Porchard, perhaps. "Officer Jinn said she saw someone running toward the Port Authority building. Head through the gatehouse and cut them off."

Gecki poked her snout out from the doorway a few moments later, sniffed the air again like she might be able to smell someone hiding, and then skulked back into the street.

"Coast's clear," she rasped. "Iskar's earned his take, I reckon. Best we avoid that gatehouse, take the long way round where it's quiet."

"Sounds good to me."

They left the street and crept through adjoining gardens of dry soil where the only plant life visible were the weeds sprouting from between the tracks in stone tiles. Not the richest of districts. The people here had more important things to keep alive than roses and daisies. The hollow bronze head of a clockwork bull had been left to rust in the corner of one yard. Sheni had seen something just like it whirring and wheezing past the storefronts earlier that day, soon after they'd landed at the port. They pulled carriages of goods scheduled for morning delivery. Victorium was known for its strange machinations. For a time, there'd been more automata on the moon than people.

Organic people, that is. Sheni wasn't prejudiced.

The city wasn't completely devoid of foliage, however. Five minutes later they emerged in a public garden as deserted as the surrounding neighbourhoods. A gnarly tree similar in species to an oak stood in the centre, its twisting branches towering past the houses flanking it to scratch at the stars peppering the quiet, coal black sky. Forming a square around it were stone planters of roses, tulips and petunias. Sheni wondered how beautiful their lush colours must look against the city's grey facade when the sun broke over the horizon.

Gecki crouched beside the gate leading out of the garden and pointed at a stocky, classically-designed municipal building with tall, narrow windows across the way.

"You see that fancy office covered in balustrades over there? Port's just on the other side of it. We get round there, we're in the clear."

"What about Iskar? Will he know where to go?"

"He knows where the ship is. He's a big boy, he'll figure it out."

Sheni peered through the bars of the iron gate. The street was wide and extremely exposed, with glow-orb lanterns positioned every dozen or so metres down its length. The air was sharp and salty due to their proximity to a port that served both the sky and sea. Large gatehouses with arches wide enough to fly a cruiser through stood at either end. Ministry officers with plasma rifles in their arms stalked the pavements in search of Rago's thieves.

"The *Silver Hart* might not be very far away," Sheni said nervously, "but we've got no chance of reaching it. Not with all those guards on patrol."

"Well we're not going *across* the street, you idiot." Gecki hissed quietly and gestured for Sheni to follow her back across the garden. "Only sensible route is over it. This way."

The reptilian scaled an ivy trellis nailed to one of the walls with ease. It wasn't just the claws on her bare hands and feet that made the climb such a breeze; the pads on her palms kept her stuck to vertical surfaces like glue. Sheni hesitantly followed her up, sensing the trellis's diamond-shaped lattice bending beneath his boots.

Gecki reached down and pulled him onto a flat rooftop. They continued further upward, climbing over humming junction boxes and brick chimneys. An iron cage installed over the glass of one foggy window performed well as a makeshift ladder leading to a slope of slate tiles, which Sheni clambered up on all fours. There they reached a narrow stretch of rooftop next to one of the gatehouses.

"See? It's easy," Gecki rasped. "All we need to do is cross this bridge and drop down on the other side."

Sheni peered over the edge of the rooftop. It was a small hop to the unmanned roof of the gatehouse, sure, but one hell of a drop to the street below. Four storeys of drop, to be exact. And the persistent mist sweeping in from the ocean was making everything damn slippery.

"I fail to see which part of your route is sensible," he mumbled. "The over bit I understand. But sensible? Nah."

"Oh, be quiet, human. Do you want to escape this city or not? It's this or crawl through old sewers. And they ain't so old they don't get used, if you catch my meaning."

Sheni shivered.

"Fine. But not all of us can chop off a shattered leg and grow a new one, you know?"

Gecki took a couple of steps backward, then a running leap across to the top of the gatehouse. She landed about as gracefully as one could expect from a giant lizard. She snapped her head back and forth, then beckoned for Sheni to follow.

He stood up with his arms outstretched for balance, took a deep breath, took an even deeper gulp, and ran toward the lip of the roof.

His boot slipped on the final tile where the rainwater hadn't drained properly.

Sheni flailed toward the nearest ornate balustrade. Gecki raced back across the gatehouse roof. She whipped an arm around his waist and caught him before he could crack his skull open on the weathered stone.

"Thanks," he sighed. "Like you said, real easy."

Gecki winked at him with her one good eye and together they crept over to the other side of the gatehouse. They were about halfway across when the sound of footsteps echoed over the cobbles.

"Get down," she hissed. "Trouble's coming."

They ducked behind the parapet and watched through its decorative holes as down on the street a figure sprinted through the mist. Sheni's breath caught in his throat. Even with his hood up, Sheni could tell it was Iskar. The lean Kerulian figure. The panicked gait. The well-worn leather spacer rags.

That, and the royally pissed off Ministry officers chasing him.

Iskar burst through the thick mist lapping over the street like the waves of the nearby ocean and approached the brass railing that ran down the length of the street. There was a small drop down the other side to a neighbourhood of ship merchants and, beyond that, the Port Authority building. But the mist must have blinded Iskar to the guards already stationed on the street. Two Ministry officers stepped out from behind mechanical carts with their plasma rifles raised before Iskar could vault to freedom.

At that range they wouldn't miss, not even with the murky visibility. Iskar reluctantly raised his hands above his head and was promptly thrown to the ground.

He raised his eyes to the gatehouse and spotted Gecki and Sheni crouching behind the parapet, but kept his mouth shut. Sheni felt Gecki's claws tighten around his bicep.

"We have to help him," he said, pulling away from her.

"How?" Gecki's grip on his arm remained steadfast. "By keeping him company in his cell? Don't be an idiot, Sheni. Iskar's done for. The best thing you can do for him is get off this rock with the brooch."

"How is that supposed to help, Gecki?"

"By making sure his sacrifice wasn't in vain. Now move while the Ministry thinks they've got their man!"

"They *do* have their man!"

"Yes, but they don't have *us!*"

They reached the far end of the gatehouse's roof. Past the balustrade was a short drop to a buttress of sorts, and then a steep slope down the buttress to the merchants' yard. Sheni slid down the side, his trousers riding up against the abrasive stone, and landed behind a stack of muddy oil tankers.

Back on the street, a bell rang out. They glanced up at the railing to find one of the guards standing beside it, pointing down at them and furiously yelling something to his squad mates.

"Oh, godsdammit," Gecki snarled. "Run!"

They sprinted out from cover just as the first plasma slug exploded against the empty cans. The bell continued to toll. They had a head start against the guards up on the street. If they could get far enough ahead, maybe – just maybe – they had a chance.

The merchants' yard was mostly deserted save for small rodents and a few old statues from Victorium's history. The orange light of glow-orbs bled from the cracked doors of workshops where merchants and ship technicians were working late. Chipped and rusty signs creaked in the gentle wind.

"My comm link," Gecki rasped as they ran. "Give it to me!"

Sheni fished the small puck out of his pocket and tossed it to Gecki. She'd left her jacket on the ship in case she needed to camouflage herself. Gecki flipped it open and speed-dialled Xotl's frequency.

"Hello, Gecki," the purple starfish said calmly, appearing as a small, flickering hologram beaming from the centre of the puck. "I trust that your retrieval of the brooch went well?"

"Oh, yes, it's a roaring success. We've been made. Extraction's gonna be hot. I need you to have the *Silver Hart's* thrusters ready to burn the second we're on board."

"Understood. But the fuel hose is still attached. You'll have to remove it before you get on, otherwise we'll be tethered to the bay."

Gecki gave Sheni a withering look.

"We won't have time to detach it ourselves, Xotl. And if we get caught, so will you! Just get out there and give the nozzle a twist. You'll be fine, it won't take two minutes. Put on the enviro-suit we got you."

Being a Xocha, Xotl had very little resistance to common viruses outside of their homeworld, Estroidea, which meant they spent almost their entire life on the ship. Sheni and Gecki had splurged what few spare credits they had on a semi-transparent outfit the starfish could wear, hoping they'd join the rest of the crew on safer operations and sit with them at the Corpse & Casket, but the ungrateful starfish hadn't worn it even once.

"Getting into that suit will take longer than you make it

sound like we have," Xotl replied in their usual deadpan tone. "And I can't take the risk without it. You know how vulnerable to infection I am."

Gecki snarled and snapped the comm link shut without ending the call. They were running past the stocky Port Authority building now, its slender office windows dark and lifeless, a soundtrack of waves crashing against the rocks to their left. A storm was on the way.

"Gods, that invertebrate needs to grow a spine," Gecki muttered. "You reckon you can get that hose off?"

"Before the guards catch up to us? I dunno, Gecki..."

They rounded the corner of the Port Authority building and cut through a row of storage sheds. There it was – the *Silver Hart*, lurking on a dark landing platform, glistening under a blanket of midnight dew. Searchlights from watchtowers lining the docks cut through the fog. Sheni could hear angry voices coming the other way. It was a small miracle the ship hadn't been clamped already.

"It's gonna be impossible to see anything," Sheni said, wincing as salt water in the wind stung his face. "If I disengage the hose while the pump's still on, it'll spray fuel everywhere!"

"So? It's not like we're paying for it."

"That stuff's flammable, Gecki. And we're taking off in a damn ship!"

But as they broke through the mist creeping across the stone pier and drew level with the nose of the ship, Sheni noticed that the fuel pipe no longer connected the pump to the tail end of the *Silver Hart*. The dispenser beside the enormous copper vat had been switched off and the nozzle hung up in the correct place.

The gormless green bowling ball known as Alan gurgled at them from inside the open airlock door.

"You're a lifesaver, Alan," Sheni gasped as he collapsed against the wall inside. "I guess you earned a share of the take after all, huh?"

"We're in," Gecki shouted into the intercom on the airlock wall. "Get this thing moving!"

The exterior airlock door slammed shut and the decontamination jets installed in the eight corners of the chamber hissed on. The ship trembled as the thrusters ignited, but even as the jets finished their cycle and the interior door of the airlock unlocked, they didn't appear to be going anywhere.

Gecki stormed up to the cockpit in a fury. Xotl spun around in their egg-cup shaped pilot's seat to face her.

"Will Iskar not be joining us?" they spluttered through the beak in the centre of their body.

"No, he got caught," Gecki yelled. "As will we if you don't take off right now!"

Xotl hurriedly spun back to their dashboard. As the *Silver Hart's* underside thrusters gently raised the ship off the landing platform, one of the guards' watchtowers shone its stark searchlight through the cockpit windows. Sheni and Gecki winced and shielded their eyes. Xotl's arms shrivelled slightly, their suckers puckering.

Xotl spun the ship on the spot and then shot it away from the city, away from the suffocating fog, punching through clouds that threatened to spark and roar.

"Skip to subspace as soon as we're clear of Victorium's thermosphere," Gecki ordered.

"Protocol dictates that we—"

"Just do it, Xotl, before I chuck you out your antiseptic airlock and fly the godsdamn ship myself!"

Xotl's five arms flicked switches and wrapped around the dashboard's three flight sticks.

"Yes, Captain..."

The *Silver Hart's* shuddering grew less severe with each layer of the moon's atmosphere it passed. Xotl triggered the skip drive just prior to escaping the moon's gravitational pull, as instructed. Their view of a handful of stars scattered around the enormous gas giant to which Victorium belonged was replaced instantly with a tunnel of pulsing, deep blue waves.

Sheni pinched the bridge of his nose and exhaled slowly.

Gecki sagged into her chair at the back of the cockpit and checked inside the brooch's velvet box. The golden brooch shined brightly. Not so much as a scratch on it.

"All things considered," she said with a wry smile, "I'd say that job went off without a hitch."

CHAPTER TWO

In the back room of the Rusty Bucket boarding house on the Corpse & Casket space station, Sheni leaned back in his creaking chair and laced his fingers together behind his head while Gecki paced back and forth impatiently.

"Come on, Peggi," he said. "What's it worth?"

Peggi Slim sat on the other side of her desk and inspected the stolen brooch with a brass-framed telescopic eye-piece. Not only the proprietor of the Rusty Bucket – a flea-infested pit-stop for only the most desperate pirates and spacers – Peggi was also the station's resident fence, buying up illicit cargo and selling it on the black market. She had contacts everywhere, from Barataria to Kapamentis, and could place artefacts in even the shadiest of auctions. Nice gal, if you asked Sheni.

She pulled the lens from her eye, pursed her lips and nodded sagely.

"It's genuine, all right. Good condition, too. I reckon I can get five thousand credits for it. Maybe more if the aristocrat's family wants to buy it back."

Gecki's scaly lips peeled back in a smile.

"Now you're talking. Five thousand credits it is."

"Hold your horses, lizard lady. Five thousand is what I'll make selling it on. That means four thousand for you. And that's a mate's rate."

Gecki threw back her head and hissed.

"Why'd you do that to me, Peggi? Now I've got five in my head!"

"It's fine, Gecki." Sheni twisted around in his seat to look at her. "Eight hundred credits each ain't anything to sniff at."

"Maths ain't your strong point, is it? There's four of us – you, me, Alan and Xotl. Thousand each."

"You're forgetting Iskar's take," Sheni replied.

"Pah! I'm not giving up two hundred credits for that chump. He got caught. It's not like he needs the money anymore, does he?"

Sheni grumbled and shook his head.

"I'm not sure we should be profiting from his misfortune, that's all."

"Hey. Guys." Peggi Slim stared at them expectantly. "Have we got a deal or not?"

"Yeah, course we do." Sheni gave her a wink. "Who else we gonna sell this stuff to, huh?"

"Exactly." Peggi smiled and rummaged about in the drawers of her desk. "Will hard credits do?"

"They most certainly will," Gecki replied, taking the proffered sack of credit chips. "Pleasure doing business with you."

"You heading to the bar?" Peggi asked as she walked them to the door.

"Can't make a trip to the Corpse & Casket without grabbing a drink," Sheni replied.

"All right. Maybe I'll see you down there. Got some crap here to sort out first."

Sheni and Gecki strolled through the lobby of the Rusty Bucket, a sparse hall of wooden planks nailed over steel girders and a staircase whose steps were half missing or rotten. They found Alan sitting on a ripped sofa reading a pamphlet on cheap cybernetic prostheses. Well, Sheni presumed he was reading it. One eye was focused on the crinkled paper while the other slowly drifted around in its socket like a terrestrial globe.

"Come on, Alan." Sheni helped the strange creature down from the couch. "We're done here. Time for our reward."

Outside the Rusty Bucket, fellow spacers hurried between the main concourse's rickety market stalls and the space station's numerous docks. A bunch of raiders in spiky leather outfits sat with their legs dangling over the edge of a shipping crate, singing and swigging from murky green bottles. Neon signs competing for real estate on the high, clumsily-erected walls flickered, spluttered and buzzed.

Gecki opened her comm link and called Xotl.

"Hey, starfish. Just sold the brooch. You gonna join us at the Corpse or what?"

"Thank you for the invitation, Gecki," Xotl spluttered, "but I shall have to pass. I hope you enjoy your drinks. After the last job, you have most certainly earned them."

Gecki shook her head as she slipped the comm link into the pouch looped around her neck. They set off toward the bar.

"Is it just me," Gecki asked, "or does Xotl seem distant? More than usual, I mean."

"Nah, it ain't just you. I hope they're not considering a change in career, you know?"

"Meh. Might not be the worst thing."

"Gecki!"

"What? We could have got caught back on Victorium if Alan hadn't detached that fuel hose. Killed, even. I know Xotl has their health issues, and I've always accommodated them, right? But sometimes it feels like they ain't pulling their weight."

Sheni said nothing. He didn't disagree, exactly. It just felt wrong to talk about Xotl like that behind their back. It couldn't be easy, not being able to leave the ship without worrying you might catch some otherwise harmless bug and die.

"What are we going to do about Iskar's share, then?" he said, redirecting the conversation.

"Iskar doesn't have a share, not anymore. But I'm guessing you've got a suggestion…"

"Well, the Ministerium won't keep him locked up forever, will they? All he did was steal a brooch, and he didn't even have it on his person when the guards caught him. So we could hold onto his share for him for when he gets back out."

"Nah. No way. Even if we put those credits aside for him, how long will it be till we get in hot water again and need to spend those credits to bail ourselves out? Besides, we don't know how long a sentence the Ministry will give him. He did steal from *them*, after all. Or where he'll get sent. He might not want credits once he's free. He might want blood."

"So the solution is to keep his share for ourselves, is it?"

"Way I see it, sooner or later we're gonna spend it on either us or the ship anyway. Might as well make it sooner."

Sheni cast his eyes up at the crooked Corpse & Casket sign hanging above its door.

"Unless we don't spend it *just* on ourselves…"

The space station's titular bar was as loud and boisterous as ever. Cephalopods and elephantine Alpha Rhoden played cards on wobbly wooden tables chipped from decades of knife-abuse. Leathery winged creatures lurked and tittered from the rafters. Clandestine deals were struck in dim corners. Scrap Rats dressed in oily overalls scampered around the tables and gnawed at stringy drumsticks. The stools lining the counter were occupied by aged regulars who spent more time in the Corpse & Casket drinking these days than they did flying their own ships.

Sheni snatched the sack of credits out of Gecki's clawed hand and marched toward Copper John, the automata bartender, with a cheeky grin plastered across his face. Gecki snarled and hurried after him.

"What do you think you're doing?"

"Eight hundred of these are technically Iskar's, yeah? But you're right – Iskar isn't gonna use them, and we'll spend them before he gets out. So we'll make sure we put them to good use instead."

Gecki tilted her head, but a small smile crept across her lips.

"That's a lot of beer, Sheni."

"There are a lot of people in the bar, Gecki."

Copper John came squeaking and wheezing down the bar toward them, his joints in desperate need of oiling.

"Oh, it's you guys. Let me guess. You want to extend your tab."

Sheni scooped up a handful of credits from the sack and sprinkled them over the counter.

"Booze all round," he said, twirling his finger in a circle.

The camera lens of Copper John's otherwise featureless head dilated hungrily.

"I think I can help with that," he bleeped.

The automata sounded a klaxon to signal that a round was on offer. The assorted pirates, raiders and die-hard spacers cheered as one. The first pints of beer to be poured were pressed into Gecki and Sheni's hands as a crowd surged toward the bar.

"To Iskar Barabba," Gecki said, raising her mug in a toast. "Wherever you are, whatever godsforsaken pit they've stuffed you into, thanks for all the drinks."

Sheni clinked his mug against hers and nodded solemnly.

"Poor guy. But it's what he would have wanted."

"And that," Old Guntho slurred, "was how I lifted the *Golden Molly* from the Zeldovich Quasar and became the richest pirate in the seventh quadrant."

Sheni laughed and wrapped his arm around the decrepit pirate's drunken shoulders. Gecki had passed out on top of another table like a slain dragon. Most of the bar's occupants were either snoring alongside her or had shuffled off to nurse impending hangovers in the quiet of their own ships.

He raised his mug to his lips, then scrunched up his face in exaggerated confusion.

"Hold on. I'm empty. Why don't I have a drink?"

A pair of spindly green arms appeared over the lip of the table, a sloshing mug of beer in each hand.

"Thanks, Alan," Sheni said, suppressing a hiccup. "So, erm, what were you saying about the biggest score you ever pulled?"

"Oh, don't listen to that codger," said the other elderly

pirate sitting opposite him. "He doesn't even remember what his ship was called. Go on. Ask him. He doesn't, does he?"

Ole Nana Sue was perhaps even more ancient than Old Guntho, though both were in possession of more wrinkles than the neck of a giant tortoise. Her eyes burned deep and dark in a face like a pickled walnut. All her teeth were chrome and her wispy white hair did little to cover the sprawling map of scars and cranial ports decorating her skull. They had about enough organic matter left between the two of them to build half a regular person, if that.

She was slamming back hot whiskey like it was *café au lait*. Her alcohol tolerance was insanely high, and Sheni doubted her species had much to do with it. Knowing Nana Sue, she'd probably taken her current liver from the last captain she robbed.

Sheni gave Old Guntho a shake, but he'd passed out.

"Nah, you want a story?" Nana Sue asked, taking ownership of the other beer Alan had brought over. "I'll give you a story." Her grin revealed rows of rotten gums. "A *true* one at that. You ever heard of the Sword of Bokata?"

Sheni shook his head, then waited for the room to stop spinning.

"Ah, it was before your species' time," Nana Sue said with a mocking smile. "Eighty standard cycles ago, now. It was the talk of all the taverns, let me tell you. Nobody thought it was real, you know. Lot of people still don't."

"What was so special about this sword?" Sheni asked, his elbow slipping against the table.

"Aside from being a priceless legendary artefact, you mean?" Nana Sue downed half of her beer in a single glug. "Well, they say that whoever wields the Sword of Bokata has the power to turn their enemies to allies with just a swing of its blade. Entire armies will fall to their knees in surrender and become willing slaves. With a sword like that, you can conquer whole planets. Systems. The galaxy, even."

Sheni snorted, which turned into a cough when phlegm went down the wrong way.

"But that bit's just a story, right? The metal might be real, but the myth ain't. No such thing as magic."

"I dunno, human." Nana Sue grinned menacingly. "I saw it do some pretty gnarly stuff. It casts a spell, all right."

"Wait, you found it?"

"Gods, yeah. Me and daft Guntho here, back when we rolled with Captain Blackspine. Tracked it down to an ancient warlord's burial temple on the arse-end of Oggra-coke-B."

Sheni leaned into his mug intending to drink from it, then exhaled for quite some time instead. He knew he was drunk when he could no longer tell whether liquid was going into his mouth or coming out of it.

"So, what happened? You sell it, live off the proceeds ever since?"

"Pah, I wish! Brought it back to camp all wrapped up in a shroud, just in case. Some idiot still managed to get himself caught up in that curse, though. Came stumbling out of the storeroom all mad and glassy eyed. Boss shot him dead. Next morning, the crew descended into full on mutiny. Everybody wanted to be the one to wield that weapon, you know? Guntho and I saw which way the wind was blowing. Got out of there with our lives and not much else."

"And the sword? Where'd that end up?"

"Hell if I know." Nana Sue shrugged and finished the rest of her beer. "Might still be there. Half the crew died fighting the other half, you see. Or whoever took over from

Blackspine might have moved it, then lost it when their ship went down. Makes no difference to me."

"Didn't..." Sheni covered his mouth with his fist. "Didn't you ever want to go back and check, just in case it's still there?"

"Nah. Already found it once, didn't we? That's good enough for me. Credits come and go. But you don't live to my age by getting yourself killed. Besides, I've got a tonne of stories just like that. You wanna hear 'em?"

Sheni mumbled woozily and let his head rest against the table.

"What I want is to fall asleep and never wake back up..."

Nana Sue cackled and shook her wispy head. She clicked a pair of mechanical fingers in the bartender's direction. He was presently mopping up a puddle of vomit from the mouth of Sleepy Pete.

"Hey, Copper John. Yeah, I'm talking to you – you see another walking trumpet in this place?" She lifted her empty mug. "We're gonna need a fresh round over here."

CHAPTER THREE

Sheni woke spluttering and gasping for air as he realised he wasn't only drowning in his dreams.

Gecki stood over him holding a bucket from which dregs of dirty water dripped. She snarled as he flailed about on the uncomfortable floor of the cargo hold. It was slowly dawning on him that after their drunken shenanigans at the Corpse & Casket, he hadn't even made it back as far as his hammock before passing out.

"Wha—?" He blinked through the water that ran down his face and stuck his shirt to his chest. "What the hell'd you do that for?"

"To wake you up, you idiot," Gecki yelled, "so I can shout at you!"

"Well if you're going to shout at me, do you mind doing it a little quieter?" Sheni propped himself up on his elbows and groaned. "I feel like a muloch took a crap in my mouth and used my head as a punching bag."

"Funny," Gecki said, squatting down on her haunches beside him and peeling back her lips so Sheni could get a good look at the saliva dripping off her sharp teeth. "That's exactly what I was planning to do to you if you didn't explain yourself."

Sheni scrunched up his face in confusion, then pointed a finger at the ceiling.

"May I?" he enquired with a wince.

Gecki grudgingly stood back so Sheni could climb to his feet. He held onto the bolts in the metal pillars for support. The cargo hold spun upside down and from side to side. He took a deep breath and avoided looking into Gecki's piercing yellow eye. His face felt hot and flushed enough without the added heat of her gaze.

"I'm not sure if I need a blood transfusion or another drink," he croaked, fighting the urge to throw up.

"You *need* to explain what we're doing all the way out in the Cluu system."

Sheni opened his mouth to reply, then snapped it shut as his sluggish brain caught up with him.

"Erm, what? Are you saying we're not still docked at the Corpse & Casket?"

"No, we're..." She hissed and grabbed Sheni by his soggy collar. "Gods, you're intolerable. Get upstairs."

"Okay, I'm going, I'm going..."

Sheni stumbled up the stairs, his boots scuffing every step he passed, allowing himself to be hauled to the cockpit by his furious reptilian captain like he were a dog that did a mess on the carpet. Xotl was in their egg-cup shaped pilot's seat up front. Alan stood holding a tiny cocktail umbrella on top of Gecki's terminal.

"Good morning, Sheni," Xotl said, spinning around. The motion didn't help with Sheni's queasiness. "How are you feeling?"

"About as robust as a soup in a sieve, thanks."

"Hiccup," Alan said, smiling.

"It's not the morning, not even by standard time," Gecki rasped. "Useless human's been out cold for twelve hours!"

"True," Xotl replied. "But it's always morning somewhere in the galaxy, I suppose."

"Shut up, all of you!" Gecki pushed Sheni toward his seat. "I didn't raise Sheni from the dead so you could make small talk. I did it so he could tell us why we're looking at *that*."

Sheni grabbed the side of his computer terminal before he could crash into it. Instead of collapsing into his chair and willing himself back into unconsciousness, he pulled himself down toward Xotl's dashboard. A nebulous brushstroke of stars glittered outside the windows.

A yellow dwarf star burned brightly in the distance. The only other cosmic body Sheni could see was a small, blue-green marble, and possibly another planetoid a few hundred thousand kilometres past that.

"What *am* I looking at?" he asked, feeling even more confused than everyone else. "It's not Earth, right? No way the old homeworld looks like that anymore."

"That planet," Xotl replied patiently, "is Oggracoke-B. A binary planet in the Cluu system. Its twin, Oggracoke-A, is the rock that looks like a moon over there."

"Ah." Sheni swallowed hard as all the blood drained from his head. "I see what's happened here."

"Do you?" Gecki grew steadily more irate. "Care to elaborate?"

"Before anyone gets angry," Sheni said, backing into the dashboard, "I ask that they consider how much they like credits…"

"I like credits a hell of a lot more when they aren't wasted on fuel for pointless trips to the other side of the galaxy!"

"Not pointless," Sheni said, wincing. "Just... optimistic."

"My apologies, Gecki," Xotl spluttered. "I rather assumed he already had your approval for the journey. I should have checked before activating the skip drive. But you didn't protest the coordinates when Sheni burst in here insisting that we leave at once."

"I was practically comatose, Xotl. That's hardly enthusiastic approval, is it? I don't even remember leaving the bar, let alone giving the go-ahead for this nonsense."

"It was moments after the two of you stumbled through the airlock singing the lyrics to the French national anthem."

"*Marchons,*" Alan gurgled.

Gecki growled deep in her throat and turned back to Sheni.

"This had better be good."

"Have you ever, erm..." Sheni tried to offer Gecki a confident smile, but it came out as more of a grimace. "Have you ever heard of the Sword of Bokata?"

Gecki tilted her head to the heavens and scraped her claws down her scaly face.

"Oh gods, is this something you heard about last night in the Corpse? Who told you the story? Was it Sleepy Pete before he had that Salandrian Slammer? Or after?"

"It was Ole Nana Sue, actually..."

"That crazy screwball? Stars above, Sheni. You *are* an idiot. You can't trust a word that madwoman says. She doesn't even remember how to string a sentence together most days!"

"Oh, come on, Gecki. That's mean. She and Old Guntho were proper hell-raising pirates back in their day."

"Maybe, but that day was the best part of a freakin'

century ago! They haven't raided anything more than a pantry since before you were born!"

"But they still have more experience than all of us combined. *Each*. If they say some priceless artefact might be just lying around for someone to grab, we'd be foolish not to follow up on it."

"Unless she was just pulling your chain. Having some fun at your expense. You humans can be pretty gullible when it comes to the galaxy, you know..."

Sheni crossed his arms and tried to look as if his head wasn't trapped between the clamps of a slowly tightening vice. Gecki rolled her eyes.

"Fine, go on, then. What's this tall tale Nana Sue weaved for you?"

"Look, I'll skip over all the nonsense about this sword having the power to bring armies to its knees, and whatnot. The important thing is that other people believe it's true. That's what gives the sword its value. Its, you know, *price tag*. According to Nana Sue, this relic will sell for millions."

"So will her recipe for apple scrumpy, if you listen to her. And I'll have you know the secret ingredient's just lighter fluid."

"Gecki, listen! Nana Sue said this was one of the biggest scores she and Guntho ever landed. Millions of credits. We're talking *Lucky Quark* money, you know?"

"Then why didn't they come back for it?" Xotl asked.

"Good question," Gecki snarled. "Sheni?"

"She said there was some kind of mutiny." Sheni shrugged. "I dunno, guys. I can't say I was in exactly the most lucid state when I heard all this, all right? All I know is they found a legendary artefact in some ancient warlord's burial temple, and the last time they saw the sword, it was here. Yeah, it's a long shot. And sure, it doesn't sound quite as genius a scheme now I'm something approaching sober. But we're here, aren't we? Isn't it worth a look?"

Gecki stared Sheni down until he was forced to lower his bloodshot eyes to his scuffed boots. When she next spoke, she did so to Xotl instead.

"What's this planet like? Let me guess, a magma-drenched death trap?"

"Remarkably unremarkable, in fact," the starfish replied. "Comfortable gravity, an atmosphere rich in nitrogen and oxygen. Largely unpopulated. And for what it's worth, this Nana Sue person gave Sheni remarkably precise coordinates."

"Precise coordinates to the middle of godsdamn nowhere," Gecki grumbled. "Everywhere has a coordinate or two. Doesn't mean anything interesting's there."

"But we won't know until we take a look," Sheni insisted. "Come on, Gecki. Where's that pirate spirit of yours? That rebellious yearning for adventure? Your—"

"Oh, shut up, human." Gecki shook her head. "Of course we're going down there. It's a stupid plan, and there's no way this magic sword of yours is still there after eighty years. Nana Sue's probably told that story to a thousand other crews. But we've already wasted the somnium, haven't we? Might as well take a field trip while we're here."

"Hell yeah! To fame and riches, right?" Sheni squeezed past her on his way to the pantry. "Just give me a few minutes while I pack myself full of electrolytes..."

He suddenly paused and clutched his stomach. Things were shifting down there like a magic eye puzzle.

"You all right?" Gecki asked with a tilt of her head.

"Better make that twenty," he groaned, rushing to the bathroom instead.

CHAPTER FOUR

It was a good thing Xotl hadn't gotten drunk with the rest of them, because for all the gusto he was putting behind their trip planetside, Sheni couldn't actually remember half of what he'd discussed with Ole Nana Sue the night before. Apparently he'd parroted off a whole series of precise coordinates before passing out on the floor of the cargo hold, however.

Oggracoke-B looked... well, *nice*.

Lush forests and tropical jungles. Deep oceans of cerulean blue. A temperate climate. The only thing stopping one of the major galactic empires or corporations from colonising it fully was its lack of proximity to anywhere else interesting. Even the twin planet with which it shared an orbit around Cluu was a bland and barren rock with nothing but a bunch of largely automated iron mines to show for itself.

The *Silver Hart* soared down through calm clouds and skimmed lakes and treetops alike. Flocks of multicoloured birds murmured over the horizon. With so much of the planet undeveloped, it was tricky to find a stable clearing with enough space to land the ship. Xotl endeavoured to find somewhere as close to Nana Sue's old pirate camp as they could.

Sheni, having recovered from his hungover ordeal in the bathroom, changed into a set of clothes that stank less of sweat and booze and joined Gecki down by the airlock. Alan stood beside the doors with his trusty red-handled wrench in his hand.

"Looks like the whole gang's ready to explore," he said, giving Gecki an enthusiastic grin.

"Not quite," Gecki rasped bitterly, raising her scaly brow towards the ceiling.

Through the slitted windows of the airlock doors Sheni watched as leaves fluttered and grasses flattened against the earth. Flimsy tree trunks bent sideways from the force of their ship's thrusters. The *Silver Hart* settled on its landing gear with a soft and spongey *thwump*.

"How far from Nana Sue's old camp are we?" Gecki shouted up to the cockpit. "Presuming it exists, of course."

"Approximately twelve hundred metres to the north."

"Ain't there nothing closer? I can't imagine all those pirates trekking back and forth each day."

"Whatever Ole Nana Sue used as a landing platform for her skiff eighty years ago has definitely been reclaimed by the jungle," Xotl replied patiently. "Apologies, but short of having you jump out mid-flight, this is as close as I'm going to get you."

"Understood. Hey, Xotl. You able to come down here for a moment?"

Sheni's shoulders sagged as he sighed.

"Leave it, Gecki. Please don't make a thing of it."

"I'm not making a thing," she rasped. "It's the principle

of it. The Xocha can't hang back and let us do all the work every damn time."

"I don't think that's how they—"

Sheni shut his mouth as Xotl came slowly cartwheeling down the staircase on their five arms. It was a rather delicate process.

"Yes, Gecki?" they asked through the beak in the centre of their body, their suckers dilating nervously.

"Suit up, starfish," she growled. "You're coming with us."

"What? No, it's far too dangerous. It'll be better if I keep an eye on the ship."

"Nonsense. This planet's harmless, you said so yourself. Barely populated. Little in the way of aggressive fauna. And the pirates who set up camp here sure as hell ain't around anymore. You're more likely to die tripping over a pebble."

"Well that hardly sounds like a pleasant experience either," Xotl spluttered. "Especially given I haven't tried out the suit yet. What if it doesn't fit properly, and it tears?"

"And whose fault will that be? We bought it for you months ago. But something quiet and easy like a walk through the trees is the perfect chance to try it out, right?"

"Go on, Xotl," Sheni reluctantly added. "It'll be great having you along with us. You're always missed. And it'll be good for you, too. Can't be healthy being stuck in the ship all the time."

"No, I can't risk catching something. Who knows what bugs and viruses are in this planet's atmosphere? It's hardly been professionally terraformed, has it? No, I'd rather make sure nothing happens to our ride out of here. Somebody has to. Maybe next time, after I've given the suit a proper inspection."

"You told us that last time…" Sheni said uneasily.

"And this time I'm saying no." Xotl's arms wilted. "Please

respect my decision. As a Xocha, you know how important it is that I protect my health."

Gecki bared her teeth as if she were gearing up for a fight, then rolled her one good eye.

"Fine. Whatever." She punched the button beside the airlock doors to open them. "I respect that your kind can't wander around as freely as we can. I respect that you need all this quarantine tech to keep us from dragging crap back onto the ship. But there comes a point when focusing on the problem when we've given you the solution is just plain rude. Come on Sheni, Alan. Let's go."

Sheni followed Gecki into the airlock. She closed the door behind them and triggered the unlocking sequence before Sheni had a chance to apologise to Xotl.

"I think you might have been a bit harsh," he said, shielding his eyes from the sun as the exterior doors hissed open.

"Nah. I was a bit honest, that's what I was." Gecki stormed out into the clearing. "Somebody had to say it, otherwise Xotl's gonna think what they're doing is normal. And it ain't, not even for a Xocha."

Sheni glanced back into the ship – Xotl had climbed up to the cockpit again – sighed, and then followed Alan down to the strip of flattened grass. Canopies rustled in the breeze. Tropical critters sang and cawed in the distance. The air smelled of pine, clay, and faint petrichor. Apart from the mosquitoes, it was pretty much perfect.

He checked the compass on his data pad, turned on the spot, and pointed north.

"Right, then. I guess we'd better start walking that way."

CHAPTER
FIVE

After a long while spent climbing over crooked roots, navigating their way around pockets of wet bracken and thick mud, and slapping mosquitoes from their necks, Sheni, Gecki and Alan finally reached what they assumed was the site of Nana Sue's old pirate camp.

Even if it wasn't, they'd stumbled across something very special indeed.

Half hidden by snaking creepers and woody lianas bridging the soil with the jungle's tallest trees was the head of an enormous stone statue. Half of its tusked face had crumbled away, and the rest was sun-bleached, cracked and covered in dried bird droppings. Below its gaze was a giant hole dug into the earth. Vines and moss and poisonous passion flowers carpeted every intricately carved floor tile, column and plinth.

Gecki leaned over the edge of the pit and sneered.

"You've never done anything to piss Ole Nana Sue off, have you? Like, said she looks like a fried raisin, or whatever?"

"Erm, not that I'm aware of, no. Why?"

"Just making sure she hasn't led us into a trap."

"Don't be ridiculous. She knows how many times I've kept Old Guntho from drowning in his own drool. Nana Sue and I get on like a house on fire."

"Yeah. You're the house, and she's the fire."

"Gregarious conflagration," Alan gurgled.

Sheni made the trek around the pit toward the giant head. It ended at the shoulders, each of which was wide enough for Sheni to climb onto should he wish to wade through centuries of animal excrement. He was hoping for some kind of interior, that maybe the pirates had set up camp above ground, but the head appeared to be made of solid stone.

"Hey, human. Over here." Gecki waved him back over. "There's steps leading down to the bottom."

Sheni returned to his crewmates and peered down at a crumbly series of steps lining the inside of the pit, winding counter-clockwise to a fern-infested hypaethral perhaps fifty metres below.

"That's a lot of steps," he said, swallowing hard, "and not much bottom visible from where I'm standing. You reckon that's where we'll find the camp?"

"Well, the old prune told you she found the sword inside the burial temple, right? Probably pitched their tents in there, too. And maybe whoever emerged victorious from that mutiny of theirs returned the sword to this warlord's resting place, you know?"

"Oh, yeah. Coz pirates are the respectful sort, always putting stuff back where they found it."

Gecki prodded Sheni forward with a claw.

"Do you want to find this treasure or not?"

Sheni carefully lowered himself onto the first step available – the *actual* first step had long since broken away – and edged his way down the crude staircase. Gecki stomped after him, one hand tracing the wall in case the steps cracked and she needed to quickly glue herself to something. Pebbles crumbled loose and tumbled into the foliage. Alan hopped down beside the two of them with the oscillating momentum of a Slinky toy and a seemingly uncomprehending smile etched across his face.

"Perhaps it was a good thing Xotl didn't come with us," Sheni said, giving the next tile a hesitant prod with his boot. "There's no way they'd make it down all these steps. I know we splurged for a good enviro-suit, but it can only take so much friction before it rips. I've snagged my trousers twice already."

"Yeah, well, don't tell Xotl that. They need to come out with us eventually, even if it's just to the Corpse & Casket."

Sheni considered this.

"Can't promise they won't get a splinter…"

Distracted, he put his foot onto the next step down without looking. It cracked apart in a cloud of rubble and dust the second he put his weight on it. Sheni would have followed it down and likely snapped his neck had Gecki not darted forward and wrapped her claws around his arm.

"The climb back up's gonna be fun," he said with an uneasy smile. That was the second time she'd saved his life in as many days.

"Let's hope the pirates left behind some supplies. It might be better if I crawl up the sides and chuck a rope back down on our way out. Here, let me test the next one."

Gecki scampered across the wall bridging the two distant steps while Sheni stood feeling as useless as a toothbrush in a Kwoo Fim colony. He could make the jump. The question was whether the stone could take the landing.

"You should be all right," she said, stomping on the stone with her strong hind legs as she continued gripping the wall with her Velcro-like pads. "Go on, jump across."

Alan bounded past Sheni like a rubber cannon ball. Gecki had to stick her stumpy tail out to keep the green idiot from tumbling all the way down to the bottom.

"A ladder," Sheni sighed. "Why couldn't the pirates have installed a ladder?"

The rest of their descent went without incident, though Sheni took twice as long making sure each platform could support him despite following Gecki, who – not that Sheni would ever mention it to her face, of course – probably weighed close to twice as much as he did. He collapsed against a stone wall engraved with an open-mouthed jungle beast as soon as they reached the bottom.

Gecki's bare foot kicked something metal. She reached into the dense ferns and came back holding an old tin mug.

"Well, your pirates were definitely here," she rasped, chucking it back into the greenery. "I suppose that's promising."

Alan, who could barely see over the top of the plants, held up someone's ribcage.

"Some of them are *still* here," Sheni mused, "by the looks of it. I guess Nana Sue was telling the truth, huh, Gecki?"

"Come on." Gecki clicked a pair of claws at him. "I don't care if you're hungover. You can't possibly need a rest, not with how slowly you took those stairs. Temple's this way."

Sheni puffed out his cheeks and followed her through the only archway in the circular pit. The rest of it was lined with more engravings, though time and nature had rendered most of them indecipherable. It must have been incredible back in its day. He wondered if the warlord ever got to see it, or if it had only been commissioned after their death.

"It's a bit dark," Gecki grumbled. "Bit smelly, too."

"Here." Sheni handed her his data pad. "Use this."

Gecki switched on its flashlight feature. Sheni pushed past her, mouth agape.

"Woah. Now *that's* what I call a tomb."

The chamber was mountainous. Pillars as wide as sequoias bore the weight of the excavated ceiling and, above that, the stone head rising from the ground. Two braziers, once aflame, stood cold atop finely carved columns, and the long pools that lined the central nave were dry and caked with rings of salt. Fish caught in the ocean must have swam in them once. Everything was veiled in cobwebs and dust, and decorated with invasive plants and the skeletons of tiny rodents.

"This warlord must have really been something," Sheni said, soaking the temple in. "I wish Nana Sue had mentioned the guy's name. Maybe she did, and I just forgot…"

"You have creepy places like this back on Earth?" Gecki asked. "In my culture, the dead are lucky to get a pile of stones and a speech goodbye."

"Yeah, a few of our cultures went pretty big when it came to honouring their dead royalty. The ancient Egyptians built massive pyramids in the desert. The actual burial chambers inside weren't that huge, funnily enough. Sometimes they were sealed up completely so no-one could find them, too, not even thousands of years later. But there were all sorts of tunnels and secret rooms to throw off thieves, you know? And if you got trapped trying to steal all the riches they were buried with, well…" Sheni shrugged. "Then it became your tomb, too."

"Saved their loved ones a few credits, I suppose. How about we try and not get stuck down here though, yeah?"

They continued toward the rear of the burial temple. Alan carved furrows through the snowlike dust as he scampered around the chamber. It wasn't only the skeletons of rodents they stumbled across. Clearly the pirates' mutiny had spread throughout the site.

Another stone statue, this one full-bodied and smaller than the bust outside, stood between the empty pools at the end of the walkway. The bipedal warrior it depicted was dressed in a full suit of armour complete with horned helmet and, judging by the way he placed his gauntlets on his hips and tilted his helmet to the heavens, was rather full of himself. Presuming it was to scale, the man was still a good couple of feet taller than Sheni. Gecki bent down and swept a film of grime off its base.

"Here lies Bokata," she read, "Chief of the Bokata Clan and... and the rest of the inscription is too eroded to make out properly. Something about reapers and followers and stuff."

"Ah, well, that makes sense," Sheni said, scratching the back of his neck. "Guess we have our warlord's name, then. Do you reckon this is where they buried him?" He took a step back from the statue. "You don't think he's *inside* that thing, do you?"

"Nah. This is just a... a what do you call it... a *cella*. Like, an altar for Bokata's clan to pay their respects. Probably worshipped the guy like a god, or something, given all the stories about his godsdamn sword. Body's gotta be kept deeper than this, right? You know, to throw off grave robbers and looters like they did in those big triangles on Earth you mentioned. Look for a door, or another staircase of some kind."

Gecki marched off to the left, taking Sheni's data pad with her and plunging him into darkness. He fished around in his pockets for an old lighter, sparked a flame, and then investigated the space behind the statue. The wall was moist and dark where vines and roots had split the stone and let in rainwater.

"I think we can safely say Nana Sue wasn't lying, huh?" he yelled out while running his hand along the wall and checking for secret buttons.

"Yes, fine, the old hag was telling the truth." Sheni could practically hear Gecki rolling her eye. "Her crew was here, sure. And it doesn't look like the place has had many visitors since."

"Ah! So you admit the Sword of Bokata is real, then?"

Gecki snorted.

"They found *a* sword, I'll give them that."

Sheni shook his head and tried pushing in one of the more protruding stones. No such luck. There'd come a time when they'd break into a place where all they had to do was pull a candlestick and the wall would spin around to reveal a treasure chest overflowing with gold, but it wouldn't be today. Still, that just meant there was something real special at the end, right? You didn't go to all this trouble just to hide a corpse. Sure, the bones of a legendary warrior could be pretty valuable, but it was what the deceased was buried with that most looters were after.

"Hey." The click of Gecki's claws echoed across the hall. "Found something."

Sheni hurried over. *Please be a button set into a plinth,* he mentally repeated to himself. He passed Alan, who was sitting on top of the Bokata statue's helmet with his spindly legs dangling in front of the warrior's face.

"What is it?" he asked, flicking his lighter closed. "A secret doorway? A weight-based puzzle?"

"Just another inscription," she rasped. Sheni's heart fell. "About as faded and incomplete as the last one, too. Reckon I can piece it together, though."

"Well, what does it say?"

"Don't get your glands in a twist," she said, glancing at him over her shoulder. "This temple's been standing for a millennium or more. It ain't going anywhere."

The inscription in question had been carved into the face of a circular cut of limestone that reminded Sheni of a sundial, only one tilted up at a forty-five degree angle. Gecki scratched away some of the dust and dirt from inside the runes with her claw.

"'I live for hours and serve only in death,'" Gecki read. "Huh. Bit creepy. Goes on to say, 'Perished come the morning, at dusk I'm reborn.' Something to that effect, anyway. What do you think that's supposed to mean?"

"It's a riddle," Sheni replied. "Man, these old architects loved their word puzzles, didn't they?"

"Course, it could just be a clan motto. Something about the fleeting nature of life and a belief in reincarnation, maybe. But yeah, I think you might be right. Got any ideas what the solution might be?"

Sheni turned from the circular pedestal and squinted through the gloom. His eyes fell on the two cold braziers sitting atop the columns.

"Fire," he said with a grin. "It only burns for a short while, and only while there's something for it to destroy. Once it burns through its fuel, it dies. It's a fire."

"Reborn at dusk could mean relighting the fire come sundown, I suppose," Gecki added. "Coz by the time the camp wakes in the morning, it's burned itself out."

"So, I'm guessing we just need to light those two braziers?"

"Both of them? Nah. It's got to be more complicated than that. It's a dark room, right? If it were that simple, people might stumble across the solution accidentally."

"We have to choose one, and only one." Sheni nodded thoughtfully. "Okay, so the riddle says it's reborn at dusk. Like, sundown. And the sun sets in the west, right?"

"If you say so. Can't say I've checked."

He took his data pad back from Gecki and used its compass to find due west. Then he returned to the braziers. They were positioned so as to be perfectly in line with Oggracoke-B's magnetic poles. That had to be the solution, right?

"Let's hope there's still something in there to burn," he said optimistically.

Sheni carefully climbed the column using its intricately chiseled stone leaves and narrow trims for purchase. It would have been a lot easier for Gecki to get up there, but she remained standing by the pedestal, watching him with her arms crossed.

"Smells funny," he yelled down from near the top. "Sort of like rotten eggs."

"Probably some kind of gas," Gecki replied. "Whoever designed this place probably piped it up from the caverns below. Be careful. I bet it's extremely flammable."

"I should hope so." Sheni covered his mouth with his shirt and stuck his lighter through a gap in the brazier. "There's nothing else in this thing except dung and ash."

He sparked the lighter and the entire brazier erupted in blue flame. Sheni jerked his arm back, the hairs on the back of his hand already singed, and dropped to the floor. He landed on his feet, fell onto his arse, and then scooted backward from the column on his elbows as a series of leaden clunking sounds filled the chamber.

The stone tiles immediately surrounding the column dropped open on rusty metal hinges. One of the ancient trap doors snapped off and tumbled endlessly into a dark void below.

"You've got to be kidding me..." Sheni stood up and dusted off his trousers. "How'd I get that one wrong?"

"I guess Cluu sets in the east here," Gecki rasped irritably. "Good freakin' job."

"What? I thought all planets rotate counter-clockwise. Earth certainly did!"

"Of course they don't, you cretin! Didn't they teach you anything in those human schools of yours?"

"You know, I graduated before they added astrophysics to the curriculum..."

"Prograde motion," Alan giggled gleefully from the other side of the hall.

"Oh, and it should have been obvious," Sheni groaned, pointing at the statue on which Alan was sitting. "That Bokata guy's staring right at the other brazier!"

"Well why don't you try lighting that one, huh?" Gecki punched him on the shoulder. "Sure, it's a fifty-fifty chance, but maybe they give people a second try."

The clunking continued, but now it sounded like things falling apart rather than into position. The tiles of the central walkway beneath Sheni's feet trembled. Pillars of dust pirouetted from the cracked ceiling. Pieces of the barren pools began to chip and crumble away.

"Erm, Gecki? What's that?"

"That, *Sheni*, is the sound of a temple preparing to crash down around your ears. Alan, get over here – we're leaving!"

"But what about the sword?"

"Pull it out of the rubble if you really must!"

Alan hopped down from the statue. But no sooner did his tiny feet slap against the ground than a hole open beneath him. Alan bounded across the broken tiles toward Gecki even as they began to fall into the chasm below the cella, but even he couldn't defy gravity long enough to avoid being pulled down, still smiling to himself, alongside Bokata's statue and half a tonne of decrepit stone.

"Alan," Sheni cried out, rushing to the edge of the rapidly collapsing floor. "No!"

Gecki yanked him backward by his collar.

"We've got to go," she snarled. "Now!"

Numb and confused, Sheni turned and sprinted for the exit – a small sliver of light in a cavern of growing darkness. Boulders crashed down to either side of him. Iron and stone groaned together. Pillars toppled like felled oaks.

Then suddenly everything went topsy-turvy and he was falling, dropping alongside a section of floor that had subsided violently at one end. He and Gecki slid down the ramp past clumps of rock and broken cogs. Gecki went flailing over the side, but not before Sheni reached down and grabbed her arm.

Her sharp claws dug into his wrist, drawing blood, as he clung desperately to the edge of the jagged, groaning platform with his other hand.

"Don't be an idiot," Gecki rasped. "You ain't pulling me back up."

"To be fair," he grunted through gritted teeth, "I'm not pulling *me* back up, either..."

The last piece of the platform snapped loose with an almighty crunch, and together they plummeted into the dingy abyss.

CHAPTER SIX

The darkness grew darker still, a blackness that devoured all until there was no up, no down – nothing but his terrified thoughts. Sheni heard Gecki snarling in fury beside him as they plunged deeper into the earth. It seemed as if they were headed for the very bowels of the planet.

And then all of a sudden, he stopped.

The wind was knocked out of him. Frigid water surged into his lungs to take its place.

He coughed, spluttered, tried to draw breath but couldn't. Every inch of his back screamed in agony from where it had smacked into the water. It wasn't broken – he could feel his arms and legs pushing through the freezing gunk – but it felt like someone had flogged him with a whip. Chunks of stone crashed into the water all around him, brushing past his boots as they sank.

Sheni wouldn't sink. This couldn't be the end, not here in some forgotten temple on a planet nobody even considered interesting enough to colonise. This tomb had enough corpses already.

His head pounding, his lungs burning, Sheni kicked upwards, praying that a piece of floor didn't land directly on top of him, splitting his skull and pushing him down, bleeding and unconscious, into the endless depths.

He thrashed, he flailed, but with his eyes open or shut, there was no way of knowing if he was even headed in the right direction...

Sheni broke the surface, felt cold air envelop his face. He was only sure his head was above water when he gasped for air and didn't drown. The world above was as black and oily as below. Once the panic of survival subsided somewhat, he heard more splashing, more crunching as rocks broke off the walls.

He looked up. A tiny pinprick of grey light from where the temple had been. Infinitely distant and unreachable.

"Gecki?" he screamed. "Alan? You there?"

No answer. Just more splashing and crashing and distant metallic groaning. He slowly turned around in the water. The cavern could have just as easily ended a few inches from his face as continued on for miles. There was only the abyss. He may have survived the fall, but it hadn't done him much good. There was no way out. He was trapped, destined to drown down there alone.

"Guys, can you hear me?"

The response came not vocally but as an orange flame in the black gloom. For a moment it flared as bright as a nuclear missile detonating in the cosmic void. Sheni's eyes took a few seconds to adjust. Alan stood on a rocky bank roughly a dozen metres away, a blank smile on his face and a flaming torch in his hand. Sheni presumed the scaly lump lying beside him was Gecki.

Exactly where the little guy had found something dry and flammable in these sodden depths, Sheni hadn't a clue, but he knew better than to look a gift Alan in the mouth. He swam across as quickly as his exhausted body permitted and crawled up onto the rocks beside him.

One look into Alan's wayward eyes, shimmering amber under the flickering fire-light, and Sheni promptly coughed up a lungful of dirty cave-water.

"Urgh. Well, if I wasn't sober before…"

He gave the scaly lump a prod. The reptile hadn't moved since he swam over.

"Oh God, Gecki. Is she…?"

"I'm not dead," she croaked. "Just freakin' exhausted. You've really gone and done it this time, human."

"Hey. How was I supposed to know the temple couldn't survive its own booby traps? It's not like it fell apart on Nana Sue or those other pirates."

Gecki slowly sat up and scratched the scales on the back of her neck.

"Yeah, well, ancient warlords loved to turn everything into a godsdamn death trap. What else were they supposed to spend all their gold on?"

Sheni squinted through the murk. The light from Alan's torch carried remarkably far, but it still couldn't reach the other side of the cavern, let alone where its ceiling used to be.

"Reckon you can climb back up those walls?" he asked Gecki.

"Maybe. It's all slick as hell, though, so I wouldn't bet on it. And I don't really fancy another fall. We're lucky it's a subterranean lake under here and not one of those gas pockets. Watch where you wave that torch, Alan."

Alan giggled to himself and then retreated further up the stony shore. The light bathing Sheni and Gecki grew slowly dimmer. They glanced at each other.

"Hey, Alan," Sheni said, his feet slipping through the loose rocks as he rose. "Wait up!"

At the top of the shore was a narrow fissure in the rocky wall of the pit. A pile of bones and cloth scraps lay beside it. Alan was already halfway through. Gecki shrugged at Sheni, and they squeezed through behind him.

The tight space stank of damp soil and sodden leaf litter plus, faintly, more of that ominous rotting egg smell. The mould spotting the wall so close to Sheni's face sent him into an unexpected coughing fit. In the midst of this, he suddenly arched his back and sucked air through his gritted teeth.

"You all right?" Gecki asked, poking his shoulder with her claw.

"Yeah, I'm fine." He exhaled slowly. "Just pulled something in my back when I hit the water."

"Ah. You're old."

"I'm younger than you!"

"Not in proportion to lifespan, you're not."

They emerged into a fresh cavern, this one untouched by the temple's collapse. Sheni rubbed his aching spine as he stared around at the ancient architecture. High walls adorned with stone skulls and cryptic runes. Steps leading up to a wide, root-ravaged archway. It was no different from the carvings and statues and pillars they'd seen upstairs – just a lot deeper underground.

More torches sat in iron brackets bolted to the wall beside the fissure. Sheni plucked a couple free and used Alan's to light them, then passed one to Gecki.

"Something tells me we're on the right track. You reckon this is where we'd have ended up anyway, had everything not broken?"

"Maybe." Gecki sneered at him. "Or maybe this is the

punishment for a different trap. Where those who fail riddles are sent to die."

Sheni climbed the steps and cautiously peered through the archway. There were three dark paths forward to choose from.

"Some kind of maze, do you think?"

"Labyrinth," Gecki said, correcting him. "Mazes are for hatchlings. Labyrinths aren't supposed to be solved. They're supposed to kill you before you reach the end."

He stepped forward as if to cross the archway's threshold, then quickly drew his foot back. There were almost certainly traps waiting to be sprung.

"Okay, we need to be smart about this, you know? Work as a team. I say we stick together, figure out—"

Alan sprinted down the central of the three corridors, giggling gleefully and tapping the ancient stone walls with his wrench.

"Gods alive," Gecki groaned. "So much for taking things carefully."

"Ah, he'll be all right, won't he? He bounces, remember?" Sheni scratched the back of his neck. "I guess it's just you and me, then."

"Yeah, and I say we follow Alan. For this path, at least. Idiot usually knows where he's going."

Sheni squinted through the gloom. All three paths were equally dark and blank.

"It's as good a guess as any," he sighed, shrugging.

They tiptoed along the nondescript corridor, their torches highlighting the cracks and pockmarks in the stone. No carvings here. No riddles to solve. Just dust and cobwebs and fossilised droppings. Their footsteps echoed into emptiness.

"I know I've said it already," Sheni whispered, "but good

thing Xotl didn't come with us, right? They'd be screwed. Never would have survived that fall."

"Why not? We did."

"Yeah, but Xotl can't swim, especially in that enviro-suit."

Gecki paused in the dark corridor.

"What do you mean, Xotl can't swim? They're a... you know... a starfish."

"Yeah, but they're not *actually* a starfish just coz they've got five arms, are they? They're a Xocha, who don't go in the water much. You're thinking of the Estroideans, the guys they share their homeworld with. They're the wet ones."

"Xotl seems pretty wet to me," Gecki grumbled.

They reached the end of the path. Alan was nowhere to be seen. He hadn't even left footprints in the dust and dirt. One corridor led off to the left, the other to their right. Both were about as un-promising as the other.

"Is it gonna go on like this forever?" Gecki snapped.

"At least it's just the two options this time," Sheni replied. "Which way, do you reckon?"

Gecki turned on the spot, studying every path, including the one leading back to the cavern.

"We go left," she eventually snarled.

They both went left. Unfortunately, Sheni and Gecki had different notions of where 'left' was.

"Where are you going?" his reptilian companion rasped. "Obviously I meant *my* left, you imbecile."

"Hey, I'm fine with whatever. Your left's as good as mine."

He turned back toward the other corridor. But the moment he took a step in the other direction he felt one of the stones in the floor sink under his boot. An iron portcullis slammed down in front of him from a gap hidden in the ceiling, separating him from Gecki.

They tried rattling it, lifting it open from the bottom, even squeezing Sheni through one of the larger gaps in the latticed grille, but there was no getting through. He was stuck.

"Godsdammit," Gecki groaned. "I figure we're all making our own way through this labyrinth, then."

"Keep heading in that direction," Sheni said, gesturing the opposite way to the subterranean lake. "We should both end up in the same place eventually, right? Unless, you know, we get stuck or hit a dead end."

Gecki nodded tiredly.

"Just watch where you put your feet, yeah? Who knows if there's a whole other bottomless pit beneath this."

"There'd better not be," Sheni muttered to himself, casting the glow of his torch over the stones. "How much deeper can this place get?"

Gecki was nothing but a distant orange glow emanating from around the next corner by this point, so Sheni set off down his own corridor alone. Shadows retreated and stalactites dripped. He kind of wished he'd run into Alan somewhere along the path. Hopefully not impaled on a bamboo whip trap or sliced in half by circular saws hidden in the walls, though.

Or bitten to death in a pit of snakes, for that matter. Sheni shivered. He'd watched a tonne of old adventure movies back on Earth, and no matter how old the crypt, there was *always* a giant nest of serpents somehow still alive to terrorise the hero.

Good thing he was no hero, then...

He turned the corner – heading right, toward what he hoped was the labyrinth's exit – and almost fell into one of those pits he was so worried about. Only this one wasn't full of snakes, nor their skeletons. Just a dozen sharpened stakes. The wooden ones hadn't fared half as well as those carved from stone, but there were still enough spikes left over to impale anyone who fell in. The shattered skeleton whose pelvic bone formed a ring around the central stake was proof of that.

"There must have been a trap here once," he said out loud to himself in a bid to break the eerie silence. "Probably fell apart over the centuries, you know, like the puzzle upstairs."

The decoy tiles hadn't completely fallen away, however. A narrow ledge bridged Sheni's side of the trap with the corridor beyond. He gave it a nervous kick. Seemed stable enough. He carefully sidled across, inch by inch, the toes of his boots sticking out over the edge. Tiny bits of stone crumbled away and sprinkled the bones like winter-grey fallout.

Metal, slamming down hard, somewhere deep in the caverns. Sheni clasped wildly at the stones at his back, trying to hook his fingers into their cracks, almost dropping his torch in his desperation to remain upright and unperforated. He steadied himself and caught his breath. Another portcullis elsewhere in the labyrinth, most likely. Perhaps not all of the traps were as broken as this one. He hoped Gecki and Alan were all right.

Safely on the other side, Sheni took every step as carefully as he could, prodding each tile and stone before putting his full weight on them, sweeping his torch across the walls in search of hidden arrow traps or flamethrowers. He covered about ten metres every minute, and it only took one of those before he was drenched in nervous sweat. He wished he weren't alone. The only thing worse than slowly dying in this place would be dying and his friends never knowing what happened to him.

Another right, then a left, then two more rights. He found a rucksack barely visible under a tent of spider webs. He gave it a kick in case it was hiding a trigger of some kind, but it clattered over without setting off anything except Sheni's allergies.

Another right. Surely he was going around in a big circle. He'd lost his bearings at the last junction. He turned left at the next one, just in case, then tried another left, but arrived at a dead end. He retraced his steps and took a right instead.

Well, he certainly hadn't come this way. Before him lay a skeleton as large as a buffalo. Whatever it had once been, Sheni sure wouldn't want to run into it while it still had flesh on its bones. He couldn't tell from the corpse whether it had been bipedal or walked on all fours. An iron collar, no longer holding onto much, was chained to the nearby wall.

"How long did they expect their snarling sentry to survive down here?" Gecki said inches from his ear.

"Stars above," Sheni said, clutching his chest. Gecki's grinning snout poked through the bars of a window set into the wall to his right. "You can't just blurt out something like that. Build up to it, you know?"

"Oh, you reckon me whispering hello would have scared you any less?"

He returned his gaze to the skeleton. Some kind of glorified guard dog, huh? Hell, it could have been a muloch for all Sheni knew. The horns on the skull sure looked big enough. He wondered who left it behind – Bokata's clan, or the pirates.

"How's it going on your side?" he asked.

"Almost got crushed by another gate," she snarled, "and

some of the floor ain't as sturdy as it used to be. But I'm pretty sure the exit's just a few turns that way. Hopefully your route joins up somewhere..."

"Yeah, well, be careful. If this were my tomb, I'd stick a few extra-nasty traps right at the end. You know, just for a laugh."

"I'll keep that in mind. Good luck..."

Gecki slipped away from the window, and Sheni crept past the skeleton. It sounded like he was headed in the right direction. A guard dog has to guard something, right? And now he knew where Gecki was going, he just needed to keep his bearings.

Right at the next junction, so he was headed parallel to Gecki. Presuming she hadn't deviated from the course, that is. Another right, and then a left...

And then a dead end.

That was fine, he told himself. It was a maze, after all. Most ends were of the dead variety. Either that or they looped back on themselves. Which the only other path available to him did. He found himself staring at the exact same skeleton lying on the floor, precisely next to the barred window through which Gecki had spoken to him.

He must have missed something. Sheni followed the path to the right again, and then the left...

...but no, there was still nothing waiting for him at its end but exactly that – an end. Three walls of hard, uncaring stone. No doorway, no way to turn except back on himself.

"You're freakin' joking," Sheni said, pacing back and forth. "This can't all be a wrong turn. Nah, it just can't. What am I supposed to do, head all the way back to the start? It's not like I can go Gecki's way. So, what? Is everyone who takes the left corridor doomed? Nah, come on..."

He clenched his jaw and pulled at his hair.

"You can't build a labyrinth without an end. You just can't!"

Alan and Gecki were right on the other side of that wall. He could feel it in his gut. They were so close to escaping this madhouse of a tomb together, but he'd never get out because he'd gone *exactly where Gecki told him to*. Why was he getting punished for the lizard not knowing her left from her right, huh? And as for Alan, well, if he hadn't gone and run off like that...

Sheni scrunched his eyes shut and wracked his brains for an answer. He had a suspicion Ole Nana Sue had tried telling him about the various traps and riddles in this place, only he'd been too hammered to comprehend a word of it. He mostly only remembered the beer. Even the thought of last night's grog made him teeter on the verge of throwing up.

A half-remembered quote rose from the depths of his cloudy, ale-addled mind...

Even when you feel like life's got you trapped, sometimes you gotta keep pushing forward.

Mad ramblings of a senile old pirate? A vacuous idiom lifted from an inane office poster? Or the secret to escaping this godforsaken maze?

Only one way to find out...

He approached the corridor's dead end, placed his hands on the far wall, and pushed as hard as he could. It didn't budge, no matter how much elbow grease he put into it. Of course it didn't. It was a damn wall. The wall of a labyrinth, of all places. They weren't exactly supposed to move.

Only this one did.

Barely at first. But a few pieces of grit fell loose as the wall shifted, and then it rolled backward with a limestone-grinding lurch. Concealed gears clunked as they turned. The corridor grew steadily longer, inch by inch, like Sheni were stretching space-time itself. And then it stopped, presumably short, with only a foot of darkness leaking through from the other side.

He eyed the gap dubiously. He could squeeze through that, right?

Sheni sucked in his gut and crammed himself into the opening. The coarse stone threatened to scrape the skin off his nose, but he fit – just about. He popped out through the gap like a cork, lost his balance, and crashed onto the filthy floor. But when he looked up from the rubble, he smiled. Alan and Gecki were lounging on a set of broken steps in an ornately-carved chamber just like the one leading to the underground lake.

"Ah, there's the human." Gecki smiled as she picked old seeds out of her teeth. "So kind of you to join us."

"Did *you* have to push open a secret wall?" he asked between giant gulps of breath.

"Nah." Gecki got up from her step. "Mine had already collapsed. Climbed right over it. Was a breeze. Shall we?"

She pointed a claw at the rune-adorned archway behind them. Alan hopped up and down excitedly.

"Extravagant internment," he spluttered.

"Heaven help me," Sheni said, deflating. "Please don't tell me we've got more deadly puzzles to solve. I don't think I've got the body or the brain for it anymore."

"Don't be so glum." Gecki picked Sheni up by the collar of his shirt and shoved him forward. "It's Bokata's burial chamber, misery-guts. We found it."

CHAPTER SEVEN

When Sheni died, he'd be lucky to be stuffed into a wooden crate previously used for transporting fish guts and spaced out the airlock. A brief salute from Alan as he shot toward the nearest sun, maybe.

This Bokata fellow had spent more on himself in death than Sheni could expect to splurge in his entire lifetime.

The tall pillars of the *cella* upstairs were back, only now their runes and carvings were lined with gold leaf that shimmered and swam an angry orange under the scrutiny of Sheni's torch. The ceiling was about as high as before, too, and he couldn't help thinking about how many thousand tonnes of rock just waited to collapse on top of them. It had been painted with what Sheni guessed to be scenes of Bokata's achievements as a warlord, but the colours were faded, the details obscured with age, and a few sections had crumbled away completely. To his left and right were vertical-slitted alcoves, far out of reach, and he wondered if sunlight had once been reflected down from the surface. Directly in the centre of the burial chamber, atop a short flight of steps on all sides, was a stone sarcophagus, surprisingly plain in appearance, apparently undisturbed.

Alan was already standing on top of its lid, brandishing his red-handled wrench aloft like he were Bokata wielding his legendary sword. Gecki prowled the chamber's perimeter in search of two things – more traps primed to kill unwitting intruders, and dusty relics to steal.

Fortunately, any traps had already been sprung by Nana Sue's old pirate crew. *Unfortunately*, the same crew had made off with any valuables the burial chamber once possessed. Their skeletons littered the dusty floor. Swords and knives still protruded from their ribs; old pistols and rifles remained clutched in bony hands. Raider rags and empty wooden crates and the tattered ruins of tents filled every corner. This must have been where they set up camp having navigated the tomb's various puzzles and riddles… which meant this was likely where all the madness and mutiny had started, too.

Sheni and Gecki reconvened with Alan beside the sarcophagus.

"It's not very fancy," Sheni said. "Maybe Bokata ran out of cash building this place and couldn't afford to put the cherry on top, you know?"

"Or maybe it's yet another trap," Gecki rasped. "We open that coffin and the floor caves in. Again."

"Or *maybe*," Sheni added, "it's a ploy to throw people off. Like, no way would Bokata go to all this lavish expense on a temple honouring his ego and then stuff himself into a plain lump of stone, right?"

They both stared at the coffin. Alan's wayward eyes stared at pretty much everything else in the chamber.

"Guess we'll have to open it to find out," Sheni said, shrugging. "Give me a hand with this, will ya?"

Sheni and Gecki got a hard grip on the lid and pushed. Not that his added weight would have made shifting the lid any more difficult, but Alan hopped off and added his own newton of force to the equation all the same. Grey limestone scraped against grey limestone like a pestle grinding grit in a bowl.

The stone lid crashed off the side of the coffin with a dull crack.

Slowly, uneasily, the three of them peered inside.

A brittle skeleton dressed in a rusty, dull, silver suit of armour lay on a bed of fine grey powder, which Sheni took a second to realise had probably once been the occupant in question.

"That," he said, covering his mouth so as not to accidentally inhale anyone, "is an extremely old body. You reckon it's Bokata?"

"I'll tell you what it isn't," Gecki snarled. "A godsdamn sword. I told you, didn't I? I mean, who finds a priceless sword and then leaves it behind?"

"I dunno, maybe the same sort of pirates who put the coffin's lid back after they were done? Look. Somebody left a note."

'Left a note' was putting it kindly. The culprit had pinned a fragile scrap of brown-spotted paper to the warlord's tarnished armour using a rusty dagger with a crooked wooden handle.

"How do you know the pirates left it?" Gecki asked, crossing her arms. "Maybe Bokata was buried like that. Maybe there never even *was* a sword, huh?"

"Because the writing's still legible," Sheni replied, raising an eyebrow as he plucked the dagger from Bokata's chest plate. "And the note looks barely eighty years old, let alone a thousand or more. Besides, who asks to be stabbed after they're dead?"

"Better after than before," Gecki grumbled. "Go on, then. What's it say?"

Sheni carefully held the paper sideways and blew away the dust and dirt. He was worried the note might disintegrate along with it. The ink was bleached out, the grammar was terrible and his translator implant gave him a headache trying to decipher the scratchy handwriting, but eventually he was able to make some sense of it.

"To the cowardly Captain Blackspine," he read. "If you're reading this, you may be wondering where your precious sword has gotten to." Sheni glanced up pointedly at Gecki, who rolled her one good eye. "Well, it ain't your sword no more. Me and the lads reckon it deserves a real leader, one who ain't so quick to shoot his own kind. We've taken what's left of the crew to Port Providence—"

Gecki reared back her head and hissed in furious laughter.

"Pah! No way. No freakin' way."

"Why? What's so terrible about this Providence place they mentioned?"

"Maybe I'll tell you if we ever get out of here. Read the rest."

"If you want it so bad," Sheni continued, the paper wilting backward as he reached the bottom, "come and earn it at the Shrine of Kismet. You'll bend the knee to the sword or I'll use it to take your head. Choice is yours. Signed, your former first mate, Flinthawk."

He delicately folded the note up and slipped it into his pocket.

"Charming. Figure this Flinthawk guy led the mutiny,

then. Clearly he's the one who had the Sword of Bokata last."

"Yeah, unless someone stole it from him. A priceless artefact like that can change hands a lot in eighty years, you know."

"Sure. But it's a start, ain't it?"

"No, it ain't. A start would be escaping this freakin' crypt before we become relics for the next unlucky raiders to plunder."

Sheni's mind returned to the labyrinth. Surely there had to be more exits and entrances than just the ones leading to the burial chamber and the subterranean lake. Otherwise, what was the point in it? No way were they climbing back up that pit, that was for sure. But navigating that maze again and all three of them making it out the other side alive… that he wasn't so keen to bet his life on.

"I'm sorry, guys. This is my fault, getting us stuck down here. I screwed up. But we'll figure something out, right? Like we always do. Maybe you can climb up those window shafts, Gecki? Or we could use the tools the pirates left behind to hack our way through the walls in the maze. Unless, you know, you've got any other bright ideas?"

"Yeah, you melodramatic halfwit, I do." Gecki sighed, exasperated, and pointed to the helical series of steps tucked away in a dark tower on the far side of the chamber. "I was thinking we could take the stairs."

CHAPTER EIGHT

The long and winding stairs were old and unstable, but eventually they led back up to the *cella* from which the crew had fallen. They had to manually push aside a section of removable wall on runners that were more rust than iron and then shimmy along the ledges left behind by the collapsed floor. Finally they could ditch the flaming torches, climb out of the fern-infested hypaethral and – after a brief period spent savouring the sunlight pouring onto their upturned faces – traipse back through the humid jungle to the clearing where the *Silver Hart* was parked.

Sheni and Gecki took turns using the shower on board the ship and then everyone convened in the cockpit.

"Whole thing was a bust," Gecki explained to Xotl. "Nearly a deadly bust, too. Next time Sheni comes up with a harebrained scheme while drunk, drown him in the water recycler."

Sheni leaned back in his chair, towel dried his hair, and said nothing. She wasn't wrong. Navigating that tomb had very nearly cost them their lives, and they had nothing but cobwebs and bruises to show for it.

"Oh dear," Xotl replied in their spluttering, deadpan voice. "I am glad everybody made it back safely, however. And to rediscover the burial site of the legendary warlord, Bokata – that's still quite the find, is it not?"

"Sure, sure, alert every news network on the extranet you can find," Gecki grumbled. "Here's a newsflash for you, Xotl. Nobody cares! It's just another dilapidated ruin in a galaxy full of them. Now, this sword of Bokata's... *that's* a find. And we didn't. Find it, I mean."

"But it *does* exist," Sheni replied. "Ole Nana Sue wasn't making it up. We found a note from this guy called Flinthawk saying he took it."

"Took it where?" Xotl asked.

"Port Providence. Nobody else had found the note since Flinthawk stabbed it into Bokata's corpse, so with any luck we'll be the first people to go searching for it."

"We ain't gonna be the first," Gecki growled. "Or the second, or third, or the last, or anything! May I remind you that the *Silver Hart* is my ship? It goes where I say, and I say we don't go. Got it?"

Sheni shared a glance with Xotl's puckering suckers. Alan slowly spun around in Gecki's chair, off in a world of his own.

"What's so bad about this Port Providence place then, huh?" Sheni folded his arms and smirked at Gecki. "You got an old boyfriend who lives there, or something?"

"Pah! I wish. Are you seriously telling me you've never heard of the place before? Not even you, Xotl?"

Sheni shook his head. Xotl wilted their arms slightly in a motion those familiar with the Xocha species recognised as a no.

"Gods. The two of you need to brush up on your pirate history. Place was famous. Well, infamous. Major pirate outpost."

"Like the Corpse & Casket?"

"Nah, way bigger. Smaller than Port Sequoia on Barataria, though. Not quite a city, but a proper sprawling hive of raiders and degenerates. Natural place for someone like this Flinthawk guy to run off to, if you ask me, especially if he was expecting trouble from Blackspine."

Sheni pursed his lips in disappointment.

"The sort of place he could fence that sword, you reckon?"

"Yeah, definitely." Gecki bobbed her head from side to side. "Not that I think he would sell it, mind you. If that note you found's anything to go by, Flinthawk fancied himself the next Bokata. Course, a lot can change. A captain can't always be top dog, not even with a magic sword hanging from their hip."

"So, why don't we go check this place out?" Sheni shrugged and looked around at the crew expectantly. "I know Port Providence is probably real rough, sure, but we've got by fine in rowdy pirate ports before. And it'll only be a quick stop. We find out what happened to Flinthawk – and more importantly, what happened to his sword – and then we follow the trail of breadcrumbs from there. Right?"

Alan had maintained a steady, squeaking spin. Gecki suddenly grabbed the back of the chair, her sharp claws cutting grooves into the leather. One of Alan's eyes slowly swivelled up to look at her.

"Let me make myself clear," she snarled. "We barely escaped the Ministry's clutches on Victorium. After fencing that brooch, the plan was to take it easy for a while. You know, have some drinks, coast subspace for a bit. Figure out the next *sensible* job, a good balance of risk and reward. And despite our little excursion here, that's still the plan. We ain't hopping from system to system in search of a rusty piece of metal half-remembered by a senile pirate desperate to reminisce about her godsdamn failures!"

Sheni opened his mouth to protest, then caught the look in Gecki's yellow eye and thought better of it. Xotl, who was cradled by their egg-cup shaped pilot's seat, subtly extended a squishy arm to check the dashboard's NavMap.

"Port Providence," they spluttered. "That's on Tübanc-Six, is it not?"

"Yeah," Gecki rasped. "Not that it matters."

"It's a mere couple of hours' flight in subspace. And it's only a short detour, presuming you otherwise intend for us to head back to the Corpse & Casket. We'd expend hardly any additional fuel."

"So? We shouldn't have wasted any fuel flying out here in the first place!"

"This isn't because I asked Xotl to fly us somewhere, is it?" Sheni's shoulders sagged. "Because I wasn't trying to take over your role as captain. It was just a drunken impulse order, you know?"

"It's not that." Gecki shook her head irritably. "But it did piss me off. Do that again and I'll strand you on an asteroid."

"Then what's the issue? We've got a good lead on that sword. Finding it would make us crazy rich. So why are you so against heading to Port Providence?"

"Coz it ain't even there anymore!"

Everybody fell silent. Alan slipped off his chair with the sluggish fluidity of syrup pouring onto pancakes.

"Stars above," Sheni gasped. "The Ministerium didn't nuke it from orbit, did they?"

"No, of course not. Gods, you're an idiot sometimes. Places like that, sometimes they just run their course, you know? I guess the Ministry was involved, though, in a way. The Tübanc system fell under Ministerial law the best part of a century ago after Negoti forfeited the mining rights. They didn't clamp down on Providence straight away, but I guess a lot of captains there saw which way the wind was blowing and skipped to the outer systems, coz one day pretty much everyone just upped and left. Outpost became a ghost town long before any executors showed up."

"Okay, but that's not necessarily a bad thing, right?" Sheni looked between Gecki and Xotl. "Flinthawk might have left behind a clue as to where he went next. Or maybe the sword's still there! Plan's no different than before, only now there won't be anyone to stop us!"

Gecki laughed.

"Oh, there will be."

"How? You said it was a ghost town."

"Yeah. A ghost town buried under a high security Ministry prison."

"Oh."

"Ah." Xotl clacked their beak nervously. "This might prove to be an obstacle."

"Will it?" Sheni threw up his hands. "Come on, guys. So what if they built a prison on top of Providence? It's not like we're talking about breaking into the penitentiary or anything. The outpost is still intact, right? Like, mostly?"

"So they say." Gecki crossed her arms and squinted at him. "They used some of it for the prison's foundations. The rest they didn't bother to bulldoze. But it is literally under the prison, Sheni. Not sitting in its shadow, or whatever. *Actually* underneath a million tonnes of sentry turrets, convicted felons and super-concrete, you get me?"

"Yeah, I hear you." He distractedly tapped his fingers against the terminal beside him. "I just don't see how sneaking into a deserted sub-basement settlement can be all that dangerous, you know? Not if we're quiet. And think of the potential reward, Gecki!"

"Sheni. Listen to me. I didn't narrowly escape the Ministry on Victorium just to waltz up to one of their prisons and ask to be arrested. Drop it."

"I think we should do it," Xotl said, much to both their surprise. "We ought to swing by the planet on our way back to scout out the site at the very least, don't you agree?"

"Look who suddenly decided to grow a spine," Gecki rasped. "No, I don't agree, Xotl. It's all well and good you saying we should risk life and liberty to find some old relic that probably isn't even on the planet anymore when *you'll* be tucked safely away in this ship."

Sheni sighed. *Here we go...*

"Don't get started on that again, Gecki. Xotl does their job."

"Yeah, and nothing else! Where were you on Victorium when we needed you, huh? I'll make you a deal, starfish. We can go to Port Providence and comb through the rubble for this stupid sword *if* you agree to strap into your enviro-suit and join us."

"You know I can't do that, Gecki," Xotl insisted. "I'm too susceptible to infection. Even the mildest virus might kill me."

"You'll be in the suit!" Gecki snarled in exasperation. "For the love of... You'll be fine, Xotl. The suit was specially designed to work with Xocha physiology. It's got five arms and everything."

"Yes, but no precaution is one hundred percent fool-proof, and I have to be especially—"

"Of course it ain't foolproof, you floppy bottom feeder, but that's life!"

"—careful these days, what with cases of nano-viruses escalating…"

"I haven't met many Xocha over the years, Xotl, but you're the only one who completely refuses to engage with the rest of society. Why even leave your homeworld if you're just gonna sit in a cockpit all the time?"

"Hey, Gecki." Sheni rose from his chair. "Dial it back a little, will ya? Xotl has their reasons for being cautious…"

"Yeah, but they ain't good ones!"

"I still enjoy travelling the galaxy," Xotl spluttered meekly. "And it's safer for the rest of the crew if I remain on the ship, too…"

"Safer for us? Pull the other one. It was only yesterday that your risk aversion put us in danger, remember?"

"I would be a liability, Gecki…"

"You're a godsdamn liability *now!*"

"I'm dying, all right?" Xotl's arms deflated over the sides of their chair. "I am dying."

Gecki snapped her scaly mouth shut. Even Alan's smile – a permanent fixture – seemed to falter slightly.

"What?" Gecki rasped quietly. "What do you mean, you're dying? Look at you. You're fine."

"For now, yes. But I have entered the final stage of my species' life cycle."

"I'm so sorry, Xotl." Sheni approached the pilot. "Is there nothing a Xocha doctor could do?"

"No. It is an unavoidable natural process."

"How long have you got? If that's not too insensitive."

"Not at all, it's quite the logical question. A few years, probably. Five at the most."

Alan pottered over and gently patted Xotl on the beak.

"Will going back to your homeworld help?" Sheni asked. "I know you were banished, but...?"

"I cannot return to Estroidea, even now. And I do not wish to. My intention is to remain here with you. My family, my friends."

"Are you still okay to pilot the ship?" Gecki asked. "What?" she added in response to Sheni's glare. "I'm the captain, I have to ask! You're always welcome on the *Silver Hart*, Xotl, whether you're flying it or not."

"Thank you, Gecki. Yes, I am still capable. I shall let you know if that changes. It should be a while before my epidermis begins to calcify."

Sheni hid his shudder as best he could. Calcification. The steady decline in mobility until Xotl was unable to flex their arms, then incapable of even opening and closing their beak. Death would shortly follow. Not exactly on Sheni's top ten list of ways to go.

"I do have one request, however," Xotl continued.

"Of course," Gecki rasped. "Anything."

"We must travel to Tübanc-Six and search for the Sword of Bokata."

"Gah." Gecki reared her head back in frustration. "No, I don't like what you've done there. You've made me feel bad. Why in the stars would you want to go to that sorry lump of rock, Xotl?"

"Because Sheni does. Because Alan does, I think. And because deep down I believe you do, too, even if you haven't realised it yet. None of you are happier than when you're chasing after the next big score. It's who we are. It's what we do."

"This ain't the next big score, though. It's a... what's the human phrase? A wild goose chase."

"You won't know for sure unless you follow the clues to

their conclusion. Don't you still dream of being an infamous pirate captain, Gecki? Perhaps a Dread Pirate Queen, even? This could be your way into the history books."

Gecki observed her three expectant crewmates in rancorous silence. Finally, she bared her teeth and hissed.

"Fine, we'll go to the Tübanc system. Freakin' hell. If poring through dirt is the daft starfish's dying wish, who am I to say no?"

"Thank you, Gecki." Xotl spun around in their pilot's seat. "Inputting the coordinates now."

Sheni watched as Xotl tapped buttons on the dashboard and flipped switches overhead to bring the skip drive online. Were their arms moving slower than usual, or was it just his imagination now he knew about Xotl's condition? When he turned back to Gecki, she'd fixed her milky eye on him.

"Xotl might have your back," she snarled quietly, "but I still think we're making a mistake. Sword or no sword, Port Providence is as far as this insanity goes."

CHAPTER NINE

Sheni couldn't understand why, when there was a whole galaxy of unpopulated planets and beaches and tropical jungles on which to set up a secret pirate base, someone would ever choose to live on such a drab and damp planet as Tübanc-Six.

Craggy basalt, mossy hillocks and black soil that stretched as far as the eye could see, all slick from silver-tinged clouds that never completely stopped raining. Miles of stark monochrome mundanity. No other settlements within three days' walk of one another.

A pretty good place to build a prison complex, in other words. There isn't much incentive to escape a prison when the rest of the planet is even less comfortable than your cell. Tübanc-Six didn't even have the decency to be truly inhospitable, either, like the lava-spewing Monzeich, or Vekemorte, whose atmosphere was plagued with toxic spores. Just tragically wet and miserable.

The *Silver Hart* chugged through the dense clouds on its spluttering, scorching thrusters.

"This prison," Sheni said. He stood beside Xotl's chair.

"They don't keep tabs on who's flying in and out of the atmosphere, do they?"

"Oh, I'm sure there's a satellite logging our approach somewhere," Xotl replied. "But the planet itself isn't off-limits to civilians – not that many civilians have reason to visit Tübanc-Six, of course. We're perfectly within our rights to be here."

"Perfect."

"I will, however, need to set the ship down quite some distance from the prison. The airspace around the facility is strictly monitored. Non-essential flight paths are prohibited."

"Of course," Gecki rasped as she stomped into the cockpit. "This wouldn't be a proper *Silver Hart* job if you weren't sitting comfortably a hundred kilometres from where the action is. Let me see the NavMap."

Xotl dutifully transferred the map across to Gecki's terminal.

"Land here," she said, jabbing a claw at her screen. "Half a klick out. Make sure you approach from the north. Those rock faces should keep the *Silver Hart* hidden."

"Are you sure?" Xotl spluttered. "That's within the prison limits. We'll show up on their scans."

"Only if you fly above the cliffs. A backwater Ministry site like this can't afford ground penetrating radar. Why do you think they built the prison on top of Port Providence? To save on infrastructure costs. Just trust me, yeah? I don't want to be caught on this sodden rock any more than you do."

"Very well. You're the captain."

Sheni nodded to Gecki.

"What've you been off doing these past few hours?"

"Research," she snarled. "Someone has to. If we're

gonna do this, we're gonna do it *right*. Not accidentally bumbling into a maximum security cell block, Sheni-style. I found an old map of Port Providence on the extranet."

"You saying you know a way inside the old outpost?"

"Maybe. I guess we'll find out how accurate it is. Or how thoroughly the Ministry covered it up."

"Coming up on the landing zone now," Xotl said. "Keeping below one hundred metres."

The *Silver Hart* skimmed above the granite-scarred landscape, kicking up a fine spray of pebbles and puddle water in its wake. Despite their apparent medical prognosis, it was evident that Xotl had yet to lose any of their touch. They deftly navigated gneisses and white-speckled tors with elegant twitches of the customised dashboard's three flight sticks, coasting mere metres from the sheer cliff face of rock to their port-side before braking hard and touching down gently in its clammy shadow.

"Everybody meet at the airlock in five," Gecki snarled. "Stay on comms, Xotl, and don't let the engines cool off. We won't be gone for long."

Sheni didn't need to prepare much. He threw on his leather spacer jacket and tightened the laces of his boots. His data pad was already tucked in his pocket. He leaned against the wall beside the airlock and waited for Alan and Gecki to rejoin him. Gecki was wearing a vest jacket of her own, purely so she had a place to stash her tools.

"Ready," she snarled at the ceiling.

The interior set of airlock doors hissed open. They shuffled in, waited for the cycle to complete, and then descended the steps into a cold cloud of drizzle. The world was all grey rock and black puddles, the only plant life the weeds and thistles crawling desperately from the cracks.

The air was thin and tasted vaguely of static, but it was breathable.

"Stars above," Sheni mumbled. "It's like the Scottish Highlands, only with all the colour sucked out of it."

"Keep it moving," Gecki rasped, stomping past him. "The ship might be hidden for now, but that doesn't mean there ain't patrols. We need to be quick, and we need to be smart."

He followed her along the foot of the cliff, always keeping to its shadow, smoke-coloured soil crunching underfoot. Alan bumbled along behind. Nothing else stirred amongst the lifeless landscape. The only sound other than their own was the relentless patter of rain on rocks.

As they stepped out to navigate a natural archway, Sheni peered back the way they came. Up on the very edge of the cliff stood a rickety hut assembled from old wood and salvaged steel.

"That watch tower," he said, tapping Gecki on the shoulder. "I take it that's not part of the prison, right?"

"Nah, looks like it's left over from the old outpost. Definitely not built to regulation."

"Why's it still standing?"

"Even demolishing stuff costs credits. Especially when you're the Ministry, and everything's gotta be done by the book. Can't just go tossing dynamite around. And who knows," she added with a hiss to her voice, "maybe they still use it, so keep your godsdamn head down."

Around the archway was a steep slope of shale boulders. Each was roughly two metres in diameter and worn perfectly smooth. Easy to slip a foot between and roll an ankle. Much to Sheni's disappointment, it appeared to be the only way in or out of their present gully. He slid and scaled over each as carefully as he could. Alan hopped from one to the next like a globular frog leaping between lily pads.

"How are you feeling about Xotl?" Sheni whispered to Gecki once they'd clambered halfway up.

"What do you mean, how am I feeling? I'm fine. Xotl's the one dying, not me."

"Come on, Gecki. I know you're not that heartless."

She tilted her head down at him.

"I'm sad, all right? I've known Xotl for over ten cycles. Never considered the possibility that their species had shorter lifespans. Won't be the same without the dumb starfish flopping about the place."

"Did you mean what you said about Xotl always having a place on the ship, even if they can't fly it anymore?"

"Of course." Gecki bared her teeth. "What do you take me for? Xotl might be a cowardly fool sometimes, but they're still family. They're stuck with us until the end."

"You were talking about kicking them off the crew only a few hours ago."

"Yeah, well, that's when I thought they were just being a bit useless. Totally different."

"I suppose we'll have to think about funeral arrangements," Sheni mused. "Do the Xocha have any religious rites or burial practices we need to know about?"

"I'm sure Xotl will tell us if they do. Otherwise they'll be going out the airlock. First time that invertebrate will have used it in a decade, thinking about it. Now shut up. Prison's in sight."

Sheni heaved himself up to the top of the boulders, wiped his damp hands on the legs of his trousers, and caught his breath while soaking in the view. Xotl had kept the *Silver Hart* too low on their approach for him to get a decent look at the prison before. The giant, windowless monolith of gunmetal grey super-concrete jutting out from halfway down the cliff's sloping crown wasn't winning any architectural awards. It was almost entirely oblong and slightly longer and wider than it was tall, save for the four watch towers occupying its corners. An ugly security checkpoint stuck out from the front. Then again, they'd built it in the arse end of nowhere. The only view of it most visitors could expect to enjoy was from the inside.

"What does a person have to do to get sent all the way out here?" he asked.

"The T-6 Correctional Facility takes thieves, murderers, tax avoiders – all sorts. I reckon trespassing on prison property is probably grounds for incarceration, though. Maybe," Gecki added with a snarl, "they lock up the sort of idiots who flap their mouths right after they've *just* been told to keep quiet, too."

"All right, all right." Sheni rolled his eyes and lowered his voice. "This entry point of yours had better work. My knees are scraped to hell and I'm gonna catch a chill."

"It ain't far. And this is your job, remember, not mine."

He trudged after her, his shoulders hunched and his hands stuffed into his jacket pockets, wishing his fellow crewmates could get on the same page for once. Gecki would soon change her tune once she had a legendary sword in her claws. But they hadn't gone more than fifty metres further along the slope of gravelly pebbles toward the prison before Gecki grabbed Sheni and pulled him into cover behind a basalt stack.

"Searchlights," she rasped. "Stay still."

Despite Gecki's instruction, Sheni risked a peek. One of the security towers was lit up like a lighthouse and was sweeping its piercing, unblinking gaze back and forth across the wide, open plains of granite.

"They looking for us, you reckon?" he whispered.

"Maybe. Probably not. Could just be a precaution. Routine, even."

"You don't sound too sure."

"Pah, they'd do more than shine a light about if they thought raiders were breaking in. You see that sort of bush thing over there, just below the next outcrop?"

Sheni didn't take long spotting it. It was about the only patch of planet that wasn't as dead as a gravestone. The emaciated greenery clung to the rock like barnacles on a ship's hull.

"Yeah?"

"When I say so, we make a run for it. Keep Alan on a close leash, got it?"

Sheni nodded, grabbed Alan's hand, and waited for her signal.

"Now," she snarled as the searchlight swung away from them.

They sprinted across to the withering foliage and slammed into the screen of rock to either side of it just as the searchlight made another pass across the plains. Sheni rubbed the leaves between his fingers.

"How in the stars did something grow here when the rest of this planet's so barren?"

"It had plenty of fertiliser."

Sheni brushed the brittle vines away from the rusty iron grate beneath, then quickly jerked his hand back.

"A sewer pipe. *That's* your way into Port Providence?"

"Drop the disgusted act, Sheni." She winked at him. "This ain't the first time you've waded through dung to get what you want. What did you expect, a back door the Ministry forgot to padlock?"

"Sort of, yeah."

"I told you, the Ministerium built the prison on top of the old outpost because it was cheaper than installing all their infrastructure from scratch. Mostly that involved the water reclaimers, the geothermal heaters and – you guessed it – the sewage system."

"Which means..."

"It's still in use, even now. Yeah. Only reason the pipe's not welded up completely. I'd pinch your nose, if I were you."

"Gecki..."

"What?" She offered him a big-toothed smile. "Having second thoughts? Coz I am more than happy to hike back to the ship if this fool's errand of yours has lost its appeal."

Sheni ran his hands down his face and took a deep breath.

"Look, I know you think this is a stupid idea. But so far this is going much easier than the Victorium job, and the potential loot is *way* more valuable. We're here now, you know? What d'ya say we stop bickering and get on with becoming millionaires?"

Gecki snorted and shrugged.

"Yeah, whatever. Keep an eye out while I cut this thing open, will ya?"

She pulled the plasma torch from the breast pocket of her vest jacket and got to work slicing through the antiquated iron. Sheni kept a tight grip on Alan to keep him from wandering off and alerting half the galaxy to their presence. But from where they were hiding, he could see no Ministry cruisers scouting the sky, no prison officers patrolling the craggy steppes. The watchful eye of the security tower aside, the coast was clear.

"And we're in," Gecki snarled, carefully setting the severed grate down to one side as the searchlight washed over the lip of the outcrop.

"I'd better carry Alan through," Sheni said, picking up the gormless green menace to wear like a backpack. "Poor guy isn't wearing any... Oh."

Gecki wasn't wearing boots either.

"Yeah," she sighed, climbing into the pipe. "When you've been in the business as long as I have, you get used to wading through other people's crap."

CHAPTER TEN

Sheni burst up from the sewage pipe's maintenance hatch gasping for breath. His body struggled to decide whether it should gulp down air or spew out his guts.

Alan clung to Sheni's shoulders with the glassy-eyed demeanour of somebody being pulled from a sensory deprivation tank. Gecki clambered out last and furiously wiped her rear claws clean on the nearest stone wall.

"What are they feeding these prisoners?" Sheni moaned between violent coughs.

"I swear to the gods," Gecki snarled. "The next time you come up with one of your stupid schemes, it had better take place in a tropical paradise."

Wherever they'd ended up beneath the prison was pitch black. Unlike the rainwater, not one drop of silvery sunlight trickled down from the surface. Gecki switched on her flashlight to reveal a cramped room full of abandoned pumps and jerry-rigged mag-tape terminals, all of it dusty and defunct. Sheni set Alan down and rapped his knuckles against the side of the pipe.

"So this pipe leads all the way up into the prison, does it?"

"Yeah, in theory. The Ministry must have set up the prison's sewer lines to run into the port's old system. I highly doubt we could follow the pipe much further though, even if we wanted to. Any way in or out of the prison itself is gonna be locked down tight."

"Good thing we're steering clear, then."

"Exactly. Not that you seem to be doing all that much steering, *human*. Do you even know where we're headed?"

"Not as such, no." He scratched the back of his neck and retched as his fingers came back covered in something sticky. "I was hoping you might have some thoughts on that. You know, what with all the research you did and all."

"Uh huh. What a surprise. I get to be the brains *and* brawn of the operation, as always."

"I mean, you are the captain, you know?"

Gecki shook her head, muttered indecipherable curses to herself, and stomped out of the pump monitoring room. Sheni quickly followed, clicking on a flashlight of his own.

The next room, found at the top of a narrow stairwell of dank stone, was larger but no less abandoned, a storage unit full of plumbing parts and hardcover binders of manuals, invoices and receipts. Semi-luminous mushrooms grew from between the floorboards. A rickety wooden desk lay hidden under a tent of cobwebs. Sheni couldn't imagine pirates filling out paperwork, but he supposed that's what boatswains and first mates were for. The captains must have pooled all sorts of resources together to keep not just a ship, but a whole community operational.

The windows of the office were as cloudy as Tübanc-Six's sky. Sheni squeezed through the door Gecki had left ajar and joined his two crewmates on the balcony of a metal staircase that groaned under their combined weight.

"Extemporary undercrofts," Alan gurgled to himself.

Sheni shone his flashlight down over a street cobbled with stones from the surface and lined with surprisingly fancy two-storey buildings. The wooden beams on their facades had rotted and a few of the roofs had collapsed, but otherwise most of the houses, while overgrown with moss and fungi, were in much better condition than the properties one usually found on pirate worlds like Barataria. Lifeless neon signs advertised taverns, merchants, tailors, ship supplies, medical services and cybernetic augmentations. At the far end of the street was a much larger structure with a domed ceiling – a town hall or pirate municipal building of some kind.

Port Providence hadn't been just some debauched hideout, or a glorified roadhouse like the Corpse & Casket. It was a proper little town – shops, doctors and all.

"Why'd they build it all underground?" Sheni asked.

"Not underground," Gecki replied, shining her flashlight up at the ceiling. "Just *in* the ground. The outpost only became subterranean once the Ministry stuck a godsdamn prison over it. I guess cutting it out of the cliff made the place harder to detect from orbit, maybe? Who knows. It was a pirate safe haven. Not the sort of address you want to advertise."

"Well, it's definitely hidden now."

Sheni continued to pry and prod at the street below with the beam of his torch. Gecki eyed him curiously.

"I know what you're thinking, but I'm telling ya: there ain't gonna be anything to find down here. Port Providence has been abandoned for years. One day the pirates here just suddenly upped and left, like I said. After all the trouble he went to get it, I hardly think this Flinthawk guy would have gone without taking his sword with him, do you?"

"Depends on their reason for leaving." Sheni shrugged. "Maybe they had no choice but to drop everything and go."

"If a bunch of raiders, or rival pirates, or gods know what else attacked Providence," Gecki rasped, "don't you think they would have taken all the loot stashed here as their reward?"

"Yeah, I guess. But they might have left behind a clue as to where the sword was taken next."

"Let's get something straight, Sheni." The reptilian put a scaly hand on his shoulder. "We only got this far because I feel bad for Xotl. Unless we find out the Sword of Bokata's on sale for ten credits back at the Corpse & Casket, we ain't following this trail any further. Got it?"

Sheni stared into Gecki's blind, milky eye and felt his heart deflate like a punctured balloon. He guessed his captain had a point. They couldn't scour the whole galaxy looking for the damn thing. Especially if they'd had to wade through sewage just to make it this far.

"Yeah, fair enough."

"Good. Now, let's find this shrine Flinthawk mentioned and put an end to this lunacy, shall we?"

Sheni hurried after her down the creaking steps.

"Yeah, about that. What's a chapel or church or whatever doing in a place like this? Most pirates don't exactly strike me as the God-fearing type."

"And they ain't." Gecki contemplated this. "Well, some of them are, but the ones screaming about gods demanding blood are usually best avoided if you ask me. Nah, the Shrine of Kismet isn't a religious thing, not really. It's more of a... a symbol of good fortune, you know? Used to be fairly popular back in the day. There's a few on Barataria, too.

Myself, I've always thought it's an easy way to waste good credits. We make our own luck, pirates and spacers most of all."

Sheni spun on the spot.

"Alan, where are... Hey, Alan, get away from there!"

Their little green companion had been scaling a splintered pole from which a faded sign hung on dull chains. He stopped trying to unscrew its bolts and quickly scampered across the cobbles to Sheni and Gecki.

"We should probably keep our voices down," Gecki rasped. "Port Providence might be deserted, but the prison above our heads definitely isn't. Who knows how far up the vents our voices might carry..."

"Stay close, all right?" Sheni whispered to Alan. "This isn't the time for sightseeing. We grab the sword and then we're out of here, got it?"

Alan blinked, one eye after the other, in what Sheni took to be a sign of understanding.

They stalked through the stifling darkness, their flashlights sweeping the way clear for them, each step of their boots and claws echoing through the gloom. Port Providence hadn't been a huge colony. A couple of thousand residents at a push. Maybe even a lower population than the prison above. Sheni shone his torch through one of the stores they passed. Sacks of old grain were still inside, some of them split, their contents spilled. Everything was remarkably intact, save for what time had ravaged. No rioting. No looting. It was, like Gecki had said, as if one day everyone had simply woken up and left without warning.

Which suggested the outpost hadn't been attacked by outside forces, not just because there were no signs of damage, but because not many raiders Sheni could think of would lead an assault on a pirate stronghold and then not take the base, let alone its contents, for their own...

"When did Port Providence fizzle out?" he whispered to Gecki.

"I told you," she growled back. "Decades ago. Before my time."

"Eight decades ago, would you say? About the same sort of time Flinthawk came here with the sword?"

Gecki mulled this over.

"Yeah, probably. Within a cycle or two. Why? What are you thinking?"

"That maybe Flinthawk used the sword to convert every pirate in the outpost to his cause and then together they set off on some doomed adventure, leaving this place to gather dust."

"What, and this Sword of Bokata magically made all the infamous captains here bend the knee to some jumped-up first mate? Hardly likely. It's just a valuable relic, Sheni. Don't believe the fairy tales."

"So the timing's just a coincidence, is that what you're saying?"

"Maybe, maybe not." Gecki shrugged. "The sword ain't gonna be here either way, so it makes no difference. Hey, does that look like a shrine to you?"

Nestled between two houses on the street running perpendicular to their own was a small, lopsided hut built almost entirely from driftwood, like it had been assembled from the hull of an old pirate skiff that washed up on the planet's mafic shores. Chimes and skulls and dreamcatchers hung from the beams of the porch outside its doorless entrance.

"I mean, it doesn't *not* look like a shrine, you know?"

The ornaments hanging from the crooked veranda

jingled as they sneaked inside. A statue carved from the same grey stone from which the port had been dug stood on a short pedestal in the shack's centre. It depicted a slender, feminine-faced alien figure almost completely swallowed by a sleek, billowing hooded robe. Benches topped with ripped, tasseled cushions lined its front and sides. Never ones to practice fire safety, numerous candles had been affixed to shelves around the wooden shack. Some were little more than waxy puddles on the floor below.

Sheni cast his light up at the statue's face.

"So this is...?"

"The Lady Kismet," Gecki replied distractedly. "The personification of luck itself. I think she's based on an Oortilian's likeness, but nobody's really sure."

"And pirates offered her credits to be blessed with good fortune on their next voyage, huh?" Sheni eyed the loose coins still sitting in the bowl held in the statue's hands. "Don't mind if I do..."

Alan whacked Sheni's greedy hand with his wrench.

"Yeah," Sheni said, rubbing his hand as he stared up at the statue. "I suppose it's not worth tempting fate."

"So, Flinthawk told Captain Blackspine to find him here if he wanted the sword back," Gecki snarled to herself. "Why here specifically?"

"Common meeting point?" Sheni suggested.

"Nah. For one, look at this place. They've done the bare minimum for a shrine, haven't they? And if you were Flinthawk, is this where you'd want to take a stand against your old boss? Hardly enough room to draw a revolver. Nah, I'm thinking there's a specific reason why he mentioned the shrine and not Providence as a whole. A reason old Blackspine would have known all too well."

"You're thinking it was less an invitation, and more a threat?"

"Yeah. Or he was taunting him, maybe. Like, this is where your sword is going, and you ain't never getting it back."

Gecki stalked around to the rear of the statue and inspected it for secret buttons or compartments. Her feet left jagged prints in the dust. She squatted down on her haunches, blew hard across the floor, and grinned. Deep grooves ran from the statue to the rear of the room.

"Aha! Scratch marks. Here, give me a hand pushing this thing."

Sheni and Gecki took up position to either side of the statue and shoved it as hard as they could. Slowly it screeched backward. Sheni was drenched in sweat by the time they were finished.

They stood back. Where the statue had been, a narrow staircase descended into the earth. Sheni shook his head in disbelief.

"Pirates and their secret treasure vaults," he muttered. "Just spend your fortune on flashy hover bikes and golden toilets, guys."

Gecki shone her light down the steps.

"*Something's* gotta be down there if it's been sealed up all this time, right? Maybe this trip won't be a complete bust after all."

"Credits are credits," Sheni said with a shrug.

He followed Gecki down. Alan hopped along behind. Oil lanterns hung from hooks jutting out from the left-hand wall at ten metre intervals. Safer than relying on electric lights in case the outpost was ever hit by an electromagnetic pulse weapon, Sheni supposed. Cheaper, too.

"So, I'm guessing this secret sub-basement was something only the pirate captains and their closest allies knew about," he whispered. "Some sort of central pirate bank to safely stash their hoards, maybe? Better than keeping everything in your cargo hold like Thunderskull," he added. "Your ship goes down, and suddenly you've lost everything."

"Unless this is nothing but a hidden passageway out of the colony," Gecki replied mischievously, "and Flinkhawk was just trying to waste Blackspine's time. But nah, I think you're right. A stockpile most of the pirates in Providence probably didn't know about. Even if the Ministry showed up on their doorstep with a damn fleet, they'd never get their hands on that loot. Gods, this could be good…"

"Look who's come around to my way of thinking," Sheni said, punching the lizard on the shoulder. "Sooner or later, everything works out."

"We still have to walk back to the ship through that sewage pipe, you know…"

"The crap'll be a lot easier to stomach with a million credits' worth of gold slung over our shoulders, I reckon."

The stairwell ended at the foot of a long and narrow corridor. To either side were large storage rooms with reinforced doors and iron-grilled walls used for stashing either prisoners or treasure. Sheni's heart sank. They were all empty except for wooden crates and a few old bones.

"Looks like a few of the other captains made pretty hefty withdrawals," Gecki rasped disappointedly as she pushed open the door of the cell next to her. "Whatever went down in Port Providence toward the end, they sure got out fast."

"I think I get it now," Sheni said, laughing sadly to himself. "Flinthawk wasn't just taunting Blackspine about the sword in that note. He was telling his old boss he was coming for everything. Not just Blackspine's hoard – the lot!"

"Cheeky little traitor." Gecki pointed a claw at Sheni. "You'd better not get any ideas."

"Pfft. What have you got worth stealing?"

Gecki spread out her arms to indicate the empty cells.

"Nothing, yet."

Disheartened, Sheni pushed open the door at the far end of the corridor. His eyes lit up.

"Don't be so sure of that..."

If this was where everyone's treasure had been relocated, Flinthawk's grand heist couldn't have got very far. The arching catacombs beyond were awash with cresting waves of gold and gemstones and goodies galore. Giant oil paintings. Priceless antiques from the lost civilisations of a dozen different species. Crowns and sceptres and vases and lamps. Mountains of high-value coins. Only a few skeletons dressed in spacer scrubs spoiled the view.

"There must be tens of millions of credits in here," Sheni said in a voice barely above a whisper.

"Tens? Try hundreds." Gecki salivated at the sight of so many jewels. "This has to be one of the biggest hauls in pirate history. I owe you an apology, Sheni. You *have* done well."

"What do you say we gather up what we can before something inevitably goes wrong?"

"You read my mind."

Gecki grabbed one of the empty wooden crates and started filling it with the most expensive looking jewellery she could carry. Sheni set off deeper into the ossuary and was wondering what other secrets its solemn passages held, whether the pirates had excavated it themselves or if they too, like the Ministry, had built on what came before, when Alan shot past him in the direction of the hidden stairwell.

"Hey, where's Alan going?"

"Probably back to unscrew that sign again," Gecki rasped, waving dismissively. "Forget about him. You know what Alan's like when it comes to loot. He can't tell the difference between a diamond and a diode."

Sheni shrugged and trudged on. His boots slipped on credit chips. Stars above. All the regulars of the Corpse & Casket could share this haul and everyone would still have more money than they could spend in a lifetime. Which, in a pirate's case, wasn't always very long to begin with.

Unless you were old-timers like Guntho or Nana Sue, he guessed. Man, if they could see this...

He stopped short. A blade lay propped up against a nondescript barrel. The metal was dull and tarnished, carrying a sickly, rusty green tint, yet something told Sheni that the edge was still sharp enough to slice through flesh like a surgical laser. The handle was bronze and wrapped in cloth that had partially unravelled, browned and blood-stained like used bandages. Sheni reached out, drew his hand back as if expecting the weapon to bite, and then nervously picked it up. It was lighter than he expected. As if the blade were lifting *him*, filling his arm with a tingly, fizzy sensation and his nostrils with the odours of copper and mould...

The Sword of Bokata. It was exactly where Flinthawk said it would be.

"Gecki, I think..." He slowly turned it over in the torch light. "I think I found the sword..."

Gecki glanced up in surprise, laughed, and shook her head as she went back to sorting red beryls from garnets.

"Ha, sure! Add it to the collection. The more credits the merrier."

Sheni searched for a sheath, but he guessed it didn't

have one. They'd need to be careful transporting it. Wouldn't want to catch tetanus, or something.

He was just searching for a box to store the sword in when he heard it. A whispering, a growling, right beside his ear and yet almost out of earshot. He glanced down at the blade in his hand. No, it couldn't be. The sword wasn't *really* magical. That was just a pirate legend, a story spacers told their kids...

Then something scuttled through the riches under the next archway over, just out of view of Sheni's flashlight.

"Alan?" he whispered.

No response. Just more treasure crashing down, more rabid animal noises. Sheni whipped his torch back and forth in mounting panic, then froze.

Red eyes watching him from the deep, derelict darkness.

Sheni slowly walked backward, gripping the sword like he knew how to swing it, and tapped his captain on the scaly shoulder.

"Erm, Gecki?"

Gecki didn't look up from the chest she was plundering. "What?"

"Port Providence might not be quite as deserted as we thought."

CHAPTER ELEVEN

Gecki slowly stood up from the chest, gemstones still clutched in her claws, and snarled menacingly at the prowling entities.

More pairs of eyes, red and hungry, leered out from the darkness. If either Sheni or Gecki shone a flashlight in their direction, they vanished, flailing and crashing through the trinkets.

"What the hell do you think they are?" Sheni whispered, his right hand wrapped around the handle of the sword. "Local wildlife?"

"Tübanc-Six doesn't have any indigenous lifeforms," Gecki replied. "Nothing big like this, anyway. Nothing intelligent. Best you'll find is a bird or a rat."

"Well, I don't know how smart they are," Sheni hissed, "but whatever's down here is a lot bigger than a damn pigeon!"

Together they sidled back toward the hidden stairwell. The Sword of Bokata hardly filled Sheni with newfound bravado. It trembled in his hands. The creatures stalking them weren't just vicious-sounding. They were numerous.

Sheni counted six or seven pairs of eyes, plus glimpses of emaciated arms and legs as they darted from his flashlight, and they were creeping forward from every direction except behind.

"How'd they even get down here?" Sheni whispered.

Gecki took another step backward and put her foot through something crunchy. She risked a glance down. She was standing in the middle of what remained of a pirate. His skeleton was still wearing a spiky helmet.

"Oh, gods... I think they never left."

Sheni stared at the ghoulish figures, then at his captain, and put the pieces together.

"You think this is what's left of Flinthawk's crew?"

"Blackspine's crew, technically. But yeah. I think that freakin' sword did something to them."

Sheni's grip on the sword tightened. He studied the greenish hue of the blade. In the darkness, it seemed almost bioluminescent...

"Nah, you're being ridiculous." He let out a nervous titter. "How are they alive and kicking, Gecki? It's been eighty years."

"Nobody said they were still alive," Gecki snarled out the corner of her mouth.

The slender shapes of corpses left to hang from gallows in the hot sun scurried through the catacombs. Fingers like desiccated tree roots crept around the columns. Sheni shook his head rapidly in mounting panic.

"Nah. No way. What happened to not believing in fairy tales, Gecki, huh?"

"It's a lot easier to believe in the supernatural when it's staring you in the godsdamn face. Now shut up and get ready."

Undead or not, their watchers were growing in confidence, no longer flinching so quickly from the light. They let out raspy, guttural growls like guard dogs choking on a chain. Sheni caught flashes of a sunken eye socket, a concave rib cage, a distended jaw. He swallowed hard.

"Ready to do what?" he asked quietly.

The heel of Sheni's boot bumped into the bottom step of the staircase. Gecki bared her teeth.

"Run!"

They sprinted up the stairs, jostling past one another, knocking oil lanterns off their hooks. Behind them came the howls and screams of starving animals fighting over scraps. Sheni briefly paused at the top.

"Should we push the statue back?" he gasped.

"There isn't time," Gecki snapped, pulling him out of the shrine. "Find Alan. Close the sewer hatch behind us. It's the only way we're getting out of here alive."

Sheni turned to run back the way they came, only to yelp in terror when Gecki grabbed his arm.

"Oh, and Sheni?"

"Yeah?"

Gecki's whole body shimmered as she activated her natural camouflage ability, her scales switching from mint green to the cold grey shade of stone.

"Don't get bit."

Sheni sprinted as fast as his legs would carry him. He remembered the way back to the pipe, didn't he? He was pretty sure they'd only walked the one street to get here. Well, and then they'd made that turn to find the shrine...

He stumbled as he heard a series of banging sounds coming from back where Gecki had disappeared. There was no way she was making that much noise by mistake. The mad lizard was providing a distraction so Sheni could get Alan to safety.

That she was likely invisible to their undead assailants only dampened her heroic sacrifice slightly.

His flashlight leapt about erratically, barely lingering on any part of the pirate outpost long enough for Sheni to get his bearings. The dilapidated lodgings suddenly looked a lot darker than they had on his way in. Like they might hide something much worse than long-shrivelled sundries…

"Alan," he hissed. "Where the hell are you?"

As if summoned by black magic, Alan appeared in the centre of the street about sixty metres ahead. He was holding a flaming torch in one hand and his wrench in the other. Where he was getting these torches, or the means to light them, was anyone's guess. Sheni supposed there had to be lighter fluid around here somewhere.

"You had the right idea, getting out of there when you did," he wheezed upon reaching Alan. "Do you know the way back to the pipe? Gecki's gonna meet us there, I think."

Alan turned and pottered through the darkness, his torch casting an ethereal shield around them. Sheni hurried to catch up. There were shapes darting back and forth just beyond the flickering glow, he was sure of it. Maybe they were scared of the fire, just like they'd been frightened of his flashlight. At first.

They reached the grey stone wall housing the old pump room. Alan stopped without warning. Bent metal sheets and rusty screws littered the cobbles.

"You have got to be kidding me," Sheni groaned.

"What's wrong?" said a raspy voice immediately to his right.

Sheni spun around with his sword primed to cut a geriatric fiend in half, but standing beside him was just a particularly worn out Gecki.

"Staircase is out," he said. "Must have fallen apart after we used it. Or when someone else did..."

A bloodcurdling screech cut through the murk. The deranged pirate crew was drawing close. Gecki cursed under her breath.

"Quick, throw Alan up there!"

Sheni tossed Alan up to what remained of the metal staircase like he was shooting a hoop in basketball. The green meanie landed on his spindly feet and then stood at the edge of the balcony watching them.

"Climb up the wall, Gecki," Sheni snapped. "There's no point in both of us dying down here."

"Well, this *was* your plan."

"You're not supposed to agree, you monster!"

"Oh, shut up. I'm not going anywhere. A good captain doesn't run."

"I'd say neither do dead ones, but look what we're dealing with..."

Alan had dropped his torch on the floor when Sheni threw him up onto the stairs. Its flame crackled between Sheni and Gecki's feet. On the edge of its light lurked the malnourished freaks from the treasure-filled catacombs. They were Nana Sue's old crewmates, no doubt about it. One of them might have even been Flinthawk himself, once upon a time. But now their rags hung loose and torn, their skin was rotten and grey, their movements sharp and rabid. These pirates were nothing but walking corpses. They brought with them an overwhelming stench of mealy decay.

Sheni held the Sword of Bokata over his shoulder. Gecki brandished her claws.

"I reckon we can take them, right?" Sheni said. "Right?"

Gecki said nothing, only bared her teeth and growled.

The flame of Alan's torch withered and waned. The

monstrous figures prowled closer and closer to the broken staircase, salivating and snapping their lolling jaws, tilting their heads like curious ravens and studying their prey with sightless, sunken eyes...

The light died. The horde sprung forward.

Port Providence was filled with the rat-a-tat of rapid-fire gunshots. Sheni ducked and covered his ears. He smelled smoke, and not just from the torch smouldering by his feet. The savage creatures moved in jerking snapshots, fighting to tear Sheni and Gecki apart even as their bodies were perforated with lead. Mere seconds passed before the whole pack had been wiped out.

Half a dozen Ministry officers marched down the street and shone the blinding flashlights of their assault rifles directly into Sheni and Gecki's eyes. The two of them instinctively raised their hands in surrender. One of the guards marched forward and snatched the sword from Sheni's unresisting grip.

"I have never been so glad to see the Ministerium," Sheni sighed.

"Bunch of heroes," Gecki rasped sarcastically. "That's what I've always said."

The guards' grizzled captain stepped forward and inspected the sword. She was a Drygg, a five foot bipedal beetle, and her traditional power armour was emblazoned with the Ministerium of Cultured Planets' insignia. Both her brown carapace and her black uniform boasted a similar number of scars.

"I always knew this old outpost had its secrets," she grunted. "Trust a pair of pirates to find them. Alert the warden," she added, nodding at a subordinate. "He's gonna want to hear this."

Sheni subtly glanced up at the metal balcony. Alan was

gone. Down the sewer pipe and back to the *Silver Hart*, if he had any sense.

"Well, thank goodness you came along when you did, you know? Honestly, I don't even know how we got down here. Must have fallen through a sinkhole, or something. If you could just show us to the exit…"

Sheni winced as flashlights were shone in his face again, accompanied by the discomforting click of half a dozen rifles being readied.

"Why so keen to leave?" the guard captain replied. "We've stopped plenty of breakouts in our time, but we've never helped someone get *into* prison before."

CHAPTER TWELVE

Sheni and Gecki were escorted back through the cobbled streets of Port Providence to a pair of large, padlocked factory doors. Behind these doors was a clunky old service elevator protected by three different sets of biometric verification scanners. They rode the elevator up in silence. There wasn't much they could say which wouldn't incriminate themselves.

"A leftover from the prison's construction," the guard captain explained, detecting Sheni's curiosity. "There hasn't been much cause to use it in the decades since. Not until we heard all the screeching down in the old outpost, that is. Thought maybe a prisoner had escaped. First time for everything."

"We don't care about your stupid jail," Gecki snarled.

"Why not? You won't be seeing much else for a while."

"Hey, look." Sheni shrugged. "This is all one big misunderstanding, you know? Let us speak to whoever's in charge. We'll get this straightened out."

"Who do you think we're taking you to see, dimwit?"

The elevator grunted to a stop and two of the officers

rolled open its stiff doors. Sheni and Gecki were shoved and dragged down anonymous corridors of colourless super-concrete, the doors metal and nondescript, not a window anywhere to be seen, through a security checkpoint filled with confused administrators, outside into a short alley where the sharp rain whipped at their eyes, and finally back inside to yet another elevator, this one considerably more modern and clean. Most of the prison guards remained behind on that level. Only the Drygg captain – still carrying the confiscated Sword of Bokata – and a pair of her officers kept watch on their two captives as the elevator slowly rumbled further upward.

Their destination was a large, circular room plated with black quartz. Dominating its centre was a weathered stone desk of typically Brutalist design flanked by three angular chairs. Twinkly music played quietly in air that smelled faintly of a salty shore. A slender Oortilian with pale blue skin and a uniform of neatly pressed black cloth stood by the office's panoramic window, looking out at the craggy, stormy horizon with his hands clasped behind his back. Sheni guessed they were up in one of the prison's towers.

"Warden Hills," the guard captain said, nodding curtly. "These are the two intruders I told you about. We found them skulking down in the old pirate outpost."

"Thank you, Captain Wrett." The warden turned from the window sporting a forced smile. "I'll take it from here."

"We found this too, sir," Wrett added, gingerly holding out the sword for Warden Hills to take.

"No, you didn't," Sheni muttered. "*I* did. Finders keepers, right?"

"Not if you found it on Ministerium property," Hills replied, not taking his dark blue eyes off the sword. "What you're describing, incidentally, is theft. Which, if you need a reminder, is a criminal offence."

"And did the Ministry reimburse the pirates who built Port Providence when they stacked a prison on top of it? I know the last surviving members of the crew who originally discovered that sword. I'm sure something in your laws says the rights ought to revert back to them, yeah?"

"Give it a rest," Gecki snarled, rolling her one good eye.

Warden Hills snorted in amusement, said nothing, only carried the sword across the office and laid it carefully down on his desk.

"Names," he said with his back to them.

"What?"

"What are your *names*?" he asked again, exasperated. "And your species, please."

"Sheni Dupont. Human."

Gecki spat out a series of incomprehensible consonants. Warden Hills turned around and looked down his slitted nostrils at her.

"I'm sorry, was I supposed to understand that?"

"Gecki," she rasped irritably. "Eureptix."

"Very good. That wasn't so hard, was it? Now, explain why my officers apprehended you trespassing on Ministerium property."

"We heard a rumour," Gecki said quickly before Sheni could open his mouth, "that the Sword of Bokata was last seen in Port Providence. Didn't realise it was part of the current prison complex. Wouldn't have come knocking if we'd known."

"The Sword of Bokata?" Warden Hills snorted again. "You expect me to believe this rusty stabbing implement is the blade in the stories you spacers tell your children?"

"To the best of our knowledge, yeah."

"It must be considerably valuable, then."

"If it's the real deal, yeah. Or at least if a rich buyer *thinks* it's real."

"Fascinating."

"Sir, they weren't the only ones down there." Captain Wrett stepped forward to rejoin the conversation. "We counted six or seven others. They were violent, feral. Had to put them down. There may be more."

"Friends of yours?" Warden Hills asked Sheni and Gecki.

"Definitely not," Gecki snarled. "They were here long before we showed up."

"A rival crew, you say?"

"In a sense," Gecki rasped with a little less confidence. "Erm, we don't think they ever left the original settlement."

"The outpost from eighty cycles ago," the warden replied with the patience of a Buddhist therapist. "Which would make many of these pirates centenarians, if my maths is correct. And yet the captain here described them as feral…?"

"It's that sword," Sheni said. "The legends say it makes your enemies bend the knee. But I think it turns them into mindless zombies."

Gecki bowed her head and sighed. Warden Hills gave the sword on his desk another glance, then fixed them both with a pitiful, incredulous look.

"Yes. Sure. How about I tell you what *I* think happened?"

Sheni tried to swallow, but his mouth was too dry. He knew he shouldn't have said the Z word.

"I think," the warden said carefully, "that you came here

as part of a much larger crew. That perhaps you intended to break into my facility and compromise the safety of my staff and inmates. Somewhere along the way you stumbled across this relic and, in typical raider fashion, the rest of your crew turned on you. And now you're feeding me nonsense about magic swords and reanimated corpses in a pathetically transparent attempt to pass yourselves off as bumbling idiots rather than career criminals. How am I doing so far?"

"Swing and a miss." Warden Hills's office was as cold as the inside of a refrigerator, but Sheni still felt like he was melting. "We really are bumbling idiots. And that really is the Sword of Bokata!"

"And I will make sure to have it appraised," Warden Hills replied genially. "I appreciate a priceless historical artefact as much as the next gentleman. A Ministerial salary only stretches so far."

"Sir," barked Captain Wrett.

"Yes, yes." Warden Hills waved a dismissive hand at her. "You'll get a cut, it's only fair."

"No, sir," the Drygg replied sternly. "What do you wish me to do with these reprobates?"

"Oh. Find an empty cell for them. Process them like all the rest. And send a team back down to the ruins," he added. "If there are any more pirates or weapons to find, I want to know about it."

Sheni wriggled impotently as a prison officer locked his hands behind his back. It took both Captain Wrett and the remaining guard to subdue Gecki.

"You can't just lock us away!" he yelled. "We haven't even had a trial!"

"And I'm sure the good citizens of Kapamentis will take

to the streets in protest." Warden Hills returned to his position beside the panoramic window. "Face it, inmates. You, this sword – there's no difference. The second you step foot in my house, you all belong to me."

CHAPTER THIRTEEN

The T-6 Correctional Facility's onboarding sequence brought a whole new meaning to the term 'processed meat'.

Sheni and Gecki were wrestled from Warden Hills's office and shepherded back through the grey and dreary bowels of his facility. Even Gecki stopped struggling after a while. One raise of an assault rifle in her direction was all the deterrent they needed. Besides, where were they gonna go?

They came to an industrial security door as suitable for keeping out starships as it was people. A reptilian Krolak sat behind a sheet of bulletproof glass in the security booth beside it. One nod from Captain Wrett and the Krolak inputted a code to open the door. A klaxon screamed out. A red light flashed on the wall. The butt of a rifle to the small of Sheni's back encouraged him through.

"Easy," Sheni hissed through gritted teeth. "I'm going, I'm going..."

"No talking," one of the guards snapped, before hitting him with the rifle again.

Sheni and Gecki were separated not long after passing through the checkpoint. Sheni was dragged off down a corridor to the right, Gecki to the left. She shot him a resentful look before they lost sight of one another. It was also at this point that Captain Wrett ceased to accompany them, leaving each prisoner to be escorted by just the one guard.

Still, with his hands mag-locked behind his back and a rifle trained on the base of his skull, Sheni wasn't about to try anything stupid. He hoped Gecki was thinking the same.

Eventually he was ushered into a cold locker room and ordered to remove his clothes. He watched awkwardly as another guard departed carrying all his belongings, including his data pad and a few old credits he'd pinched from the outpost's makeshift treasury. Then he was instructed to enter the shower in the adjacent room, where healthcare workers behind a window observed him get blasted with water and sterilising solution and frigid air until he was clean. When he returned to the locker room, shivering and sore, Sheni found the same armed guard from before waiting beside the door and a bright red prisoner uniform folded neatly on the bench. At least his boots were back.

"Red really isn't my colour," he muttered as he got dressed.

And on the ritualistic humiliation went. His fingerprints were scanned. Photographs were taken of him from every awkward angle. They took a sample of his blood to check for infections he might spread to other inmates. Sheni wondered if the Ministerium could compare their records against those of the United Earth Collective, whether the UEC even *had* a folder on him. For over two hours the prison staff fussed and fiddled like he was some kind of lab animal being studied. Perhaps that was too generous, too humane. He was more like a document that needed filing away, but first they had to figure out the precisely correct folder in which he'd fit. He was their subject, their sole focus, yet the gears of the prison turned as if he weren't even there.

When they were finally done, and his wrists were mag-locked together once again, Sheni was led through yet another security checkpoint, this one marginally less capable of surviving a block of plastic explosives. An electronic buzzer rang out and the metal gate set in a wall of criss-crossing iron bars swung open for them. Sheni had attempted to keep track of where in the facility he was, at least in relation to the warden's office, but now he was thoroughly lost. The concrete floors here were dustier and dirtier, the walls were stained with suspicious dark patches, and the heavily recycled air smelled weirdly of unwashed feet. They waited inside the checkpoint for the officer on duty to buzz open the next electronically-sealed door.

It was getting noisy now. Inmates were shouting, squawking, spluttering at one another. The fluorescent lights overhead hummed and went *plink*. Speakers whined and authoritarian orders were barked out in booming monotone. The tired rattle of low-budget ventilation systems. The banging of iron bars. The crackling of forcefields.

Sheni marched out onto a catwalk on the second storey of a three storey cell block. There had to be more than two dozen cells on each floor. Automated drones fitted with stun guns patrolled the central airspace, at the bottom of which was a communal area filled with round pits and metal benches. He glanced into one of the cells he passed. A mangy canine Raklett with a deformed snout snarled back at him. The quarters weren't spacious, even for just the one occupant. Two basic bunks, one on each side-wall. At the rear, a toilet designed for multi-species use. Beside this, a wash basin that didn't look much more sanitary than the toilet.

"Stop."

Sheni did as instructed. The prison officer nodded at the drone following them and the cell door to their right buzzed open. The guard pushed Sheni through, then slammed the door shut again. It locked automatically.

"Hands."

Sheni stood with his back to the door and poked his arms through the bars. The officer removed the mag-locks. He rubbed his wrists where the handcuffs had dug into them. By the time he turned around again, the officer was already halfway back up the catwalk.

"Is this seriously the best suite you've got available?" Sheni yelled after him. "After stealing that sword off me, I would have thought the warden could at least upgrade me to a room with a sea view!"

He sagged onto one of the cell's two bunks. No blanket. No pillow. Just a long block of spongey foam. He poked a finger into the blob to see how deep it could go and sighed.

Not very.

For the next half an hour – or so he guessed, it wasn't as if they gave inmates any way to tell the time – Sheni saw nobody outside his cell, only listened to the mad babbling of his neighbours and spotted the occasional drone floating past the catwalk toward the floor above.

Then he heard footsteps.

Sheni rushed to the bars, hoping beyond reason that Warden Hills had changed his mind and decided to let them off with a warning (though not going as far as to return their priceless relic, of course – even Sheni wasn't *that* optimistic). But it was just the same officer as before, this time with a new prisoner in tow.

Gecki was shoved through the door and underwent the same handcuff-removing procedure as Sheni. Unlike Sheni, however, Gecki lashed out at the guard with her claws the moment she was released. The guard used their rifle to swat away her outstretched hand with a bone-shattering crunch and then aimed its barrel at her head until she slunk away from the bars.

The towering reptilian shook her battered hand in pain and fixed Sheni with a death glare sharper than her rows of saliva-dripping teeth.

"Oh, you *really* screwed up bad this time, human."

"How is this *my* fault?" Sheni snapped. "We're always on the lookout for a big score. This time we actually found one! How was I supposed to know the price for finding it would be getting thrown in jail?"

"The clue was probably when I told you that the big score was buried under a godsdamn prison, Sheni!"

"Well, you're the captain. You didn't have to agree to this."

Gecki raised her claws as if intending to disembowel Sheni, then stomped off to her own side of the tiny room. Sheni wished he'd kept his mouth shut. They both knew it was only Xotl's sombre confession that had convinced her.

"Do you think they've found the *Silver Hart* yet?" he asked.

"Nah." Gecki paced back and forth down the short length of the cell. "Luxury starship like her's too small and sleek to show up on anyone's scans while she's stationary. Specially under the overhang of that cliff face. Doesn't mean they ain't out there looking for it, though."

"What about Alan? Do you think he made it back to the ship all right?"

"Well, I haven't overheard the guards talking about catching a weird green gobstopper, so I'm guessing he escaped."

"Yeah, good point." Sheni sighed. "Though he would have looked quite fetching in one of these jumpsuits, don't you think?"

"Unless more of those freaks got him, of course." Gecki gave the bars of their cell a stone-shaking rattle. "What in the galaxy *were* those things, do you reckon?"

"It's like you said. They were what's left of Flinthawk's crew. Or the pirates who lived here when Flinthawk showed up with Bokata's sword, at any rate. It does something to people. I could feel it when I picked it up."

"You still think the sword did that? It ain't magic, Sheni. There's no such thing."

"How else do you explain what we saw down there, then?"

"I don't need to explain it," she grumbled. "Don't even need to understand it. I just need to avoid running into ghouls like that ever again. Which I suppose isn't all too likely, is it, seeing as you've gone and got us banged up forever."

"You know, I don't think those zombie pirates were even up and about until I held the sword," Sheni continued, lacing his fingers together behind his head as he reclined on his bunk. "I think they were trapped down in those catacombs in some kind of stasis. That's why their bodies hadn't decomposed completely. And when I picked up the sword, it woke them up."

"A wonderful hypothesis," Gecki snarled, spraying the room with saliva. "But in case you've forgotten, those zombies got wiped out, all of our loot got stolen from us by the warden, and we've been buried away in the very prison he insists we were trying to break into. So are you gonna lie there and theorise for the next ten to twenty cycles, or will you actually be any freakin' help?"

Sheni sat up on his bunk.

"Help with what? We're in a Ministry prison, Gecki. There's no sneaking our way out of this one. No buying our freedom, either. And they took my data pad. I can't even call Xotl so they can find us a lawyer. Face it. We're screwed."

Gecki growled in exasperation and turned back to the catwalk.

"Every house has its rules," she rasped, poking her snout through the bars. "We'll learn them, then we can break them."

CHAPTER
FOURTEEN

The two newest inmates of the T-6 Correctional Facility saw and spoke to no-one until the following morning when the lights of the cell block abruptly switched back on. The prison operated on a thirty hour rotation, and apparently they'd been processed just after dinner the day before. Sheni woke with his stomach howling almost as loudly as their Raklett neighbour.

"Sleep well?" he mumbled to Gecki, who was lying on the opposite bunk and staring up at the ceiling. A hairline crack ran the length of it.

"Didn't sleep," she rasped back.

A drone drifted into position outside their cell door and an alarm rang out. The door rolled open. Sheni watched as the inmates on the opposite side of their cell block dutifully filed out onto the catwalk.

"I guess it's time to go," he said, shrugging.

They left their cell under the drone's cold, steadfast gaze, Sheni still rubbing the sleep dust out of his eyes with his knuckle. Prison officers stood in each corner of the cell block. Their black helmets made telling one guard from another difficult; all Sheni had to go on was their body type. Some had more limbs than others. Everybody walked slowly in single file around the catwalk and down the steps, floor after floor. If somebody spoke, an officer shouted at them. Nobody lashed out or deviated from the line. Sheni guessed he didn't want to find out what happened when someone did.

Down on the ground floor of the cell block, amongst the benches and seating-pits, the queue stretched to a long, dark window set in one of the concrete walls. This had to be some kind of cafeteria-slash-break area. The first few inmates were already finding seats and tucking into their breakfast.

"This ain't the only cell block in the prison," Gecki rasped quietly. "I reckon the kitchens, washrooms, all that sort of basic amenity stuff connects them in the middle."

"Yeah, so?"

"Might be useful for when we break out."

Sheni was next in line. The menu was non-existent. He was handed a tray containing a bowl of gruel, a tin of milky water and a single capsule containing species-specific nutrients. Sheni wondered what would happen if he and Gecki switched pills. Maybe he'd start regrowing lost limbs and she'd grow herself a conscience.

They found a spot on a bench as far from everyone else as possible and scrutinised the food.

"I'm not sure which is closer to a liquid," Sheni mumbled. "The slop or the drink."

"Don't get used to it," Gecki rasped, pushing her tray away. "We won't be here long."

"Oh yeah? You've got some grand plan to break us out of here, do you?"

"Working on one. This prison's got to run on patterns and schedules, right? Just got to study it, understand it, then use those routines to our advantage."

"You seem unusually optimistic."

"Yeah, well, I ain't dying in this dunghole. This isn't how my story ends, godsdammit."

Sheni waved his spoon at the other inmates chowing down around them.

"I'm sure all our new friends said the same thing..."

He dug the spoon into his slop, winced at the way it dripped off the plastic utensil, and shoved it in his mouth. His body fought to spit it back out. It tasted like raw, salty eggs and had all the texture of the sewer they'd waded through. But right at that moment he'd have swallowed anything to make his stomach shut up.

"Eat up," he sighed, washing down the nutrient pill with a gulp of milk-water. "You've got a lot of thinking to do. You need all the brain-food you can get."

After breakfast everyone went back into their cells. Hours passed with nothing to do but sit and stare at the walls, or try to catch some more shut-eye, or listen to the mad ravings of their fellow prisoners. Sheni tried to guess which crimes their closest neighbours were guilty of. The Corpse & Casket had its fair share of murderers amongst its regulars, of course, but the cheap beer helped him overlook such minor shortcomings of character.

Gecki didn't speak much, just mulled escape plans over

in her mind. Aside from another brief argument over who was more responsible for their incarceration, there wasn't a great deal for them to talk about.

Then back came the drones and the remotely unlocked doors, and they were informed by a booming voice crackling from the tannoy speakers that it was time for their allocated exercise hour.

"Yard time, in this weather?" Gecki snarled. "What a freakin' luxury."

"Can we stay in our cell?" Sheni asked, though he wasn't altogether sure he could stand looking at those same grey walls any longer.

"No," the officer grunted, tightening the grip on their rifle. "Move."

And so they joined their silent queue as before, slowly winding their way through the gated corridors of the prison in single file until they passed under the turreted gantry of an open security checkpoint and arrived in a large, barren clearing toward what Sheni believed was the rear of the prison. The grounds were as hard and artificial as the compound's walls. A few weeds sprouted from between the cracks, but good luck to anyone hoping to dig their way to freedom. A wire fence ran around the clearing's perimeter. Its barbed top looked razor-sharp. A few metres past that lay the true exterior wall of the prison, a sheer face of plain concrete some twenty-something metres high. A watch tower fitted with searchlights and mounted turrets had been built in each outward-facing corner.

"Reckon you could scale that?" Sheni whispered as they strolled out into the drizzle.

"Probably. Depends how damp the wall gets. If I lost the jumpsuit, they wouldn't see me make the climb."

"What about infra-red? Heat signatures, that kinda stuff?"

"I'm cold blooded. But yeah, with all the different species coming through their doors, I doubt our hosts haven't thought of that. You'll notice they don't keep any winged species here."

"Or they just don't let them out for yard time," Sheni replied, studying the other prisoners. "I get your point, though. Escaping won't be as easy as just hopping over a wall."

"And think how big the drop is on the other side," Gecki added. "I might be able to slip and slide my way down, but you'd definitely break your neck. Nah. If we can't sneak out the door without them noticing, our best bet is probably to leave via Port Providence, back the way we came in."

"I've never been more excited to crawl through crap, you know? If we ever get out of here, remind me to show you this Old Earth film with Morgan Freeman..."

"If it ain't in 3D, I'm not interested."

They took a slow stroll along the wire fence. The other inmates gathered in their cliques. Officers watched from high balconies. Gecki nodded up at the tallest of the prison's four watch towers.

"That's the warden's office. The one with all the windows. Swanky nob's probably looking down at us right now."

"Nah. Too busy flogging my sword on the extranet, I reckon."

"Your sword?" Gecki snorted. "You had it for all of three minutes, Sheni."

"Yeah, but *he* didn't go to all the trouble of tracking it down, did he?"

"Forget it. You ain't getting it back. Our focus needs to be on leaving this place, not heading further inside."

"We could always grab some more loot from the catacombs on our way out," he suggested coyly.

"Well, if we're going that direction anyway…"

"This cannot be happening," said a voice blocking their path. "No *way* did I get shipped halfway across the galaxy just to get locked up with the likes of you."

Iskar Barabba sneered at them, as exhausted as he was disgusted. The spacer's red jumpsuit really didn't co-ordinate well with the green irises of his eyes and the blue feathers sprouting from his temples.

"Hey, man!" Sheni opened his arms wide. "Long time no see, right?"

"Quit with the nice guy act, Sheni. You left me for dead on Victorium. I served you a small fortune on a platter and you sacrificed me to clear a path for your own escape."

"Hardly a fortune," Gecki replied. "We only got four thousand credits for that brooch."

"Then Peggi Slim mugged you off. She would have given me twice as much."

"Oh, shut up, Iskar." Sheni rolled his eyes. "Peggi hates you. And don't act like you didn't know the risk attached to your own job. You're no martyr. We all ended up in the same place eventually, didn't we?"

"Yeah, and all three of us are here because of you two!"

Sheni crossed his arms and took stock of their surroundings. Iskar wasn't alone. Five other inmates had gathered around him while they spoke. Three were Kerulian. One was an emaciated insectoid and the other a tittering, weaselly creature with eyes like Alan's.

"On a positive note, you seem to have fit right into this place."

"Already got your own posse, I see," Gecki added.

"I told you I had connections, didn't I? My big brother Javik's been imprisoned here for cycles. I guess the Ministry thought it would be nice to keep the family together, huh? And boy, is he pissed at *you*."

"Don't take this personally," Gecki rasped, "but I ain't exactly scared of a Kerulian…"

Sheni took an instinctive step backward as the largest Alpha Rhoden he'd ever seen came stomping through the gathered inmates and stopped with his huge keratinous horn inches from Gecki's snout. The elephantine beast's biceps were so keen to burst out of his jumpsuit that the seams had started to split.

"Scared now, little lizard?" the giant grunted.

Gecki bared her teeth and snarled. Javik snorted like a rhinoceros. Iskar grinned with immense satisfaction.

"You do know you're two different species, right?" Sheni asked, raising an eyebrow.

"Yeah, so?" Iskar scrunched up his feathery face. "He's adopted."

"Huh. You must have had really compassionate parents, Iskar. They must be so proud."

Javik stomped toward Sheni with a furious grunt. Iskar put a hand on Javik's chest as if he had any hope of physically holding the brute back.

"Nah, not here. Too many guards. Later, when no-one's watching."

They walked off, their posse in tow, scowling and smirking. *When no-one's watching.* Sheni didn't like the sound of that. Better to bait them into doing something stupid now while *everyone* was watching.

"You know what my mother used to tell me?" he said,

nervously scratching the back of his neck. "Don't put off till tomorrow what you can do—"

Iskar spun around with a crazed bloodlust in his eyes Sheni certainly hadn't seen back when they'd been planning their heist together in the Corpse & Casket.

"Tomorrow? Pah! I swear to every god in the galaxy, you traitors won't survive the day."

CHAPTER
FIFTEEN

A klaxon rang out in the yard and everybody was shepherded back into their cells. Hours passed. Sheni's mind turned to mush. Then, just as his stomach began to complain again, it was time for lunch. More revolting slop. More headaches as their fellow inmates bickered and prison officers barked reprimands. Sheni kept an eye out for Iskar and Javik, but they weren't amongst their neighbours. They had to be housed in a different cell block. Small blessings, he supposed.

Then back into their cells they went, and another few hours passed, as grey and immovable and monotonous as the walls in which he and Gecki were stashed, and all he could do was shut his eyes and hope he drifted off someplace else…

Sheni jerked upright on his bunk as a guard whacked the iron bars of their cell with an electric baton.

"Get up."

"Dinner? Already? I don't think my digestive system can be clogged any further…"

The guard smacked the bars again.

"Did I say you could talk? It's time to go to work, ingrates."

Sheni glanced at Gecki, who shrugged.

Rules and routines, he reminded himself. *Learn them so you can break them.*

They were escorted, alongside a handful of other presumably well-behaved inmates from their cell block, back down the catwalks and through the same corridors leading to the yard. Only this time they turned left before the final checkpoint and soon found themselves standing in a stuffy workshop instead.

Fourteen prisoners stood to either side of two noisy conveyor belts. It smelled of sweat and oil. The floor was stained a dark brown-black colour. One wall was covered in the silhouettes of tools so each and every one could be accounted for at the end of a shift. At the culmination of each assembly line was a crate of completed components, which another pair of prisoners then dutifully stacked at the far side of the workshop.

Sheni and Gecki were separated and sent to two different stations. The inmates currently on shift kept their heads down as one of the masked officers on duty approached Sheni.

"You ever fixed a drive core before?" she asked.

Sheni shook his head.

"It's real simple. Look." The officer demonstrated on a component rolling down the belt. "Unscrew the port, switch out the busted cells, screw the port back on. Repeat until you run out of cells or we tell you to stop. Got it?"

Sheni nodded.

"Good." A wrench was shoved into his hands. "Get to work."

Sheni repeated the officer's instructions. He'd actually

done something pretty similar one time when the engines on the *Silver Hart* needed fixing and Alan required a spare set of hands. All the complicated repair work was being performed by more experienced inmates further down the assembly line. Maybe that was the sort of promotion he could look forward to after half a decade's hard labour...

He looked over at Gecki. She was using a tiny brush to clean the grit from between gear spokes. Sheni wondered how many shifts it would take before she got frustrated enough to stab the brush through the black visor of someone's helmet.

He coughed and raised his eyes to the smoky ceiling. The fumes from the machinery weren't clearing properly. Had to be a blockage or breakage in the ventilation system somewhere. Something to mention to Gecki when they got back to their cell. Maybe they could use it to break out.

"What do we do if we need the bathroom?" he whispered to the old Garnidian stationed next to him.

"Hold it in or piss yourself," the Garnidian grumbled. "The officers don't care which."

After hours of screwing and unscrewing lids and swapping out busted fuel cells for new ones, Sheni's hands were starting to cramp. There was no break from the boredom. Nothing else to think about.

He hadn't even made it through his first day of being a prisoner yet. And heaven knows how many years of this he'd have to put up with.

Come to think of it, how long *was* their sentence, exactly? Without a trial, without ever being actually *officially* convicted of anything, would he and Gecki ever be let out?

Or was Warden Hills content to just keep them here – off the books, so to speak – until they either died under mysterious circumstances or the warden retired having plundered every penny of the pirates' hoard?

He was still pondering this when the door to the workshop opened and Captain Wrett stomped inside. The Drygg studied the inmates' progress, then nodded at the officers on duty.

"Shut it down," she ordered. "Shift's over. Everybody back to their cells."

Sheni set the batteries he was holding down on the conveyor belt and handed in his wrench. One by one the inmates filed out of the room.

"Not you two," Captain Wrett grunted, pointing at Sheni and Gecki. "You two stay."

Sheni and Gecki looked at each other and shrugged. The officer who'd shown Sheni how to do his job hesitated in the doorway.

"Are you sure, Captain?" she asked. "They belong to the same cell block as—"

"I gave you an order, didn't I? Somebody wants a private word with these degenerates. Scram."

The last of the officers and inmates vacated the workshop. The captain returned to the doorway to check that the coast was clear.

"Maybe the warden needs some help finding the rest of the treasure," Sheni whispered to Gecki.

"Sure, we can help," Gecki rasped back. "If that imbecile waives our sentence and gives us half the loot."

Captain Wrett returned with a visitor. Two, in fact, and neither was Warden Hills. Iskar and Javik Barabba followed her in with self-satisfied grins spread across their faces. The latter could barely squeeze through the workshop's doorframe.

"You've got twenty minutes," Captain Wrett said as she left. "Don't leave a mess."

She locked the door behind her. The two brothers showed a lot of teeth. Iskar grabbed the bluntest pair of tools he could find on the wall.

"Just the two of you this time, I see," Sheni said, following a deep gulp.

"Do I look like I need backup?" Javik grunted in a voice that rolled like thunder.

"I don't know what Iskar's told you," Gecki rasped to Javik, "but it's a load of muloch dung. We teamed up for a job. Iskar got caught and we didn't. Simple as that."

"You can still have your share of the credits," Sheni offered.

"No, he can't," Gecki snarled. "We spent it all on booze, remember?"

"Ah, yeah. Well you know what, Iskar? You can take your share from what's left."

Gecki went to protest, caught the flinty look in Sheni's eye, and then hissed in frustration.

"Fine, yes, he can have his credits. Eight hundred of them, fair split."

"Oh, how godsdamn generous of you," Iskar snapped. "And how's eight hundred credits supposed to help me in here, exactly? You may as well offer me eight million for all the chance you'll ever pay me."

"Yeah," Sheni insisted, "but we *do* owe you eight hundred, you know? And we can send those credits to anyone you want once we're out of here. How about your parents, yeah?"

"They're dead," Javik grunted.

"Yeah," Iskar said with a sneer. "And reality check, guys. You aren't *ever* getting out of here, understood?"

Sheni grabbed the nearest weapon to hand, which happened to be the empty canister of an old pressure washer. Gecki hunched her shoulders and flexed her claws.

"Let's get this over with," she snarled.

The sneering Barabba brothers took no more than a single step towards Sheni and Gecki before the ventilation system wheezing overhead suffered a catastrophic collapse. A section of air duct swung down and smacked Javik on the back of his leathery head. The Alpha Rhoden sank to the concrete floor. Iskar narrowly avoided being flattened but was swallowed by the subsequent dust cloud.

"Oh gods," he said, his silhouette backing away slowly. "Not you..."

Something smacked him around the skull and he folded onto the floor beside his brother. Sheni braced himself as a dark figure approached them through the gradually dissipating dust.

Alan pottered out of the wreckage sporting a vacuous smile.

"Feculant chicanery," he gurgled innocently.

Sheni rushed forward and gave Alan a big hug. Gecki bared her teeth in an elated grin.

"Alan, you rascal," she said. "Have you been scurrying about the prison this whole time?"

He blinked blankly.

"You can't stay here," Sheni told Alan. "Iskar and Javik might have bribed the guards for some privacy, but there's no way someone didn't hear all this junk come crashing down."

"Nah, don't you get it, Sheni?" Gecki licked her teeth.

"Alan has the run of the whole facility. He's our ticket out of here, isn't he?"

"How? I'm no stranger to squeezing through tight, unpleasant spaces, but there's no way either of us will fit in those vents."

"No, you idiot." She rolled her eye and squatted down beside Alan. "Do you think you can find your way into wherever they keep all the confiscated belongings, Alan? We need you to find Sheni's data pad so we can call Xotl. If you can grab the gems they took off me as well, great – but the data pad's the most important, yeah?"

A small bubble of drool inflated and popped in the corner of Alan's mouth.

"Yeah, I think Alan understands the plan. Off you go, now. And remember: we need that data pad, all right?"

Sheni grabbed Alan like a beach ball and hoisted him up to the broken vent.

"For the love of Old Earth, don't blow the prison up."

Alan tittered vacantly, then scampered back up into what remained of the air duct.

"And find a way to unlock our cell, will you?" Sheni called after him. He looked down at the two unconscious inmates half-buried under an avalanche of grey dust and dull chrome. "When Captain Wrett comes back and finds this mess, she's gonna revoke our yard privileges for sure."

CHAPTER SIXTEEN

Alan wriggled through the prison's ventilation system like a kernel of corn through a small intestine. His bulbous eyes rubbed against the dusty panels. Rivets bumped into his head and scraped his spindly feet. Every now and again he'd giggle or titter to himself.

"Aerated duplicity," he said quietly.

The fan at the far end of the vent turned as slowly as the second hand of a clock. A grate was installed behind it. No way forward. Alan squeezed sideways and scooted down the duct running to the left. After a while he came across a grille and pressed his eye to it.

He was above the laundry room neighbouring Sheni and Gecki's workshop. Inmates were filling big vats with soapy liquid and dunking red jumpsuits and officers' bedding into them using long, wooden plungers. Captain Wrett was standing guard while she waited for the Barabba brothers to finish beating Alan's crewmates to a pulp. Somebody must have poured the wrong detergent into a vat, because the irritable captain stormed across the hall and repeatedly smacked a poor prisoner's hand with her baton.

He blinked twice and then scurried on.

Alan wasn't dumb. Quite the opposite, in fact. He simply had a rather unique way of processing the world around him. Which meant not only did he hear what Sheni and Gecki said, he understood every single word of it.

His brain just interpreted things differently. Broke things down into their basic components, then rearranged them in more efficient ways.

A grey rodent with a barbed tail came limping down the vent toward him. They stared at each other until Alan reached out and booped it on its pink nose. It squeaked and ran away. Alan paused next to a junction box and fiddled about with the wires. The fans started to cycle properly and blew some of the dust and droppings from Alan's path. Then he carried on, confidently swerving left and right as if guided by a divine hand.

Another grate in the vent. He peeked through. Officers were sitting and eating in a break room. A beverage synthesiser rattled and hummed in the corner. A few guards watched races on a holo-projector. Whichever team they wanted to win wasn't doing very well. Uh oh. Alan saw the noodles steaming in one officer's bowl and his stomach gurgled. He hadn't eaten anything for almost a whole rotation.

closer

Fifteen minutes later and Alan smelled petrichor. Whoops. Somehow he'd shot right past the security division and reached the exterior wall overlooking the prison yard. Drizzle descended on the deserted concrete. Guards continued to man the watch towers in each corner of the prison. Raindrops dripped from the metal grille.

fallacious trajectory

Alan savoured the comparatively fresh air and then

wriggled back the way he'd come. At least he'd already swept his path clear of grime. Eventually he came to a room devoid of anything except a short bench and a few lockers. It smelled of feet and bleach. A bit more wriggling and he arrived above a shower room. A dozen more metres down the duct and he overlooked a large cluster of shelves stocked with all manner of personal items, from folded clothes to jewellery to a prosthetic arm with concealed knives and a shotgun undercarriage.

proximate placement

Smiling ever so slightly wider than usual, Alan slid down the chute and pried open the grate set amongst the tiles in the storage room's floor. Its screws were old and rusty, and it came loose easily. The room was deserted, its door presumably locked. He pottered down the aisles, jumping up and down to see the labels affixed to the higher shelves.

His smile faltered. He couldn't find anything referring to a Sheni or a Gecki. Maybe someone else's data pad or comm link would do. Of course, electronics that had been in storage for a while might not have any charge left, and Sheni would be sad not to get his old jacket back…

The groan of squeaky hinges. Alan froze, then poked his head around the shelf. There was a guard in the adjacent room – a small cubicle from which said guard could unlock the storage room or open the nearby checkpoint gate. Luckily, the octopod was only rearranging themselves in their chair. They had a mudball game playing silently on the monitor installed in the corner of the ceiling.

Alan shushed himself and kept looking.

There was a stack of boxes on the table directly beside the storage room's reinforced door. New Arrivals, according to their labels. Alan climbed the plastic leg and pulled himself up onto the tabletop.

Sheni's data pad, plus a handful of credits, rested upon his neatly-folded jacket, t-shirt and trousers. Gecki's jacket lay next to it. He searched the latter's pockets but he didn't find any gemstones. The guards had probably confiscated *those* items rather more permanently. He looked around the room for a sack and found one he liked – it was a good one made of soft velvety fabric with a fancy lace drawstring – and scooped everything inside, including a glass eye that had been rolling about on the table. You know, just for good measure.

He was about to leave when he smelled it.

Fresh fruit.

Licking his lips, Alan approached the door to the security cubicle. The guard's attention was still utterly captivated by the game on the screen. A big, juicy kwagua berry sat on the desk beside them. Rarely capable of facing the same direction at once, both of Alan's eyes rolled hungrily toward it.

He tiptoed across the floor, stopped inches from the officer's creaking chair, and reached up for the fruit with a gangly green hand...

The guard spun around with their tentacles raised, but the cubicle was empty. Sighing cantankerously, the octopod swivelled round to watch their game again.

Back inside the vent, Alan wolfed down the entire fruit in six bites. He let out a tiny burp. Then he remembered why he'd been in the storage room in the first place.

Step one, get Sheni's data pad. Check.

Step two... call Xotl for help?

Alan prodded the screen of the data pad with a mucky

finger until it opened a comm channel with the *Silver Hart*. The call was answered after just a few musical pulses.

"Hello," Xotl spluttered. "What in the stars is happening? You've been gone for—"

"Non-compliant durance," Alan gurgled.

"Alan, is that you? What are you doing on Sheni's data pad?"

"Vamoose succour."

"Put him on the line, I have no idea what you're—"

"Subjugate poltroonery," Alan said firmly, ending the call.

He smiled to himself.

Mission complete. A job well done.

Alan tucked the data pad into his bag and dragged it back toward the workshop. He'd only gone a few minutes before he heard a set of familiar voices echoing through the ducts. Pushing his face against the next grille in the vent he passed, Alan smiled. Captain Wrett was escorting Sheni and Gecki back to their cell.

"You expect me to believe that bunch of muloch dung?" the captain asked, somehow looking even more rugged and pissed off than usual.

"Yeah, like I said," Sheni replied, scratching the back of his neck. "Javik grabbed a hammer from the tool wall and tried swinging it overhead. Idiot brought the whole duct down on top of himself."

"Yeah, sure. And Iskar?"

"Got knocked out by Javik as he fell," Gecki quickly rasped. "Clumsy guy."

"Stars above," the captain sighed. "Lock these two morons up. And if you breathe a word of this to anyone," she added, "I'll make sure your next visit's with someone considerably less incompetent. Got it?"

Gecki mimed zipping her scaly lips shut as another prison guard escorted her and Sheni out of Alan's view.

Of course. Alan's eyes rolled counterclockwise in thought. Sheni had told him to unlock their cell door so they could get out. He could probably find his way back to their cell and drop the data pad through the bars in the vent hatch, but that only solved half the problem, didn't it? Xotl wasn't likely to bust through the doors of the prison any time soon.

Alan tapped the side of his head with his wrench as he formulated a plan. Dribble pooled on the floor of the vent.

"Omnipresent scrutiny," he whispered proudly to himself.

He scampered and squeezed his way further along the vent, following the path down which Sheni and Gecki had been led. They were headed back to their cell block. Alan knew from his time scouting out the prison that all the essential amenities were, as Gecki had earlier surmised, installed in the facility's centre. That included the primary Control Room. The cell doors, the drones, the security checkpoints – everything could be operated manually from inside that command centre.

It was definitely the shiniest part of the prison Alan had seen, he knew that much.

It was also one of the hardest to find. Alan wasn't the best at telling the time, what with not wearing a watch, but more than half an hour must have passed before he was in position above the Control Room. He hoped Sheni and Gecki weren't too disappointed in him.

Three uniformed security officers worked in the room below, each in a sunken pod surrounded by camera monitors. There was only the one guard using the computer terminal Alan reckoned he needed, but the four-armed

Luethian was practically glued to it. There was no way to distract them, not from up in the vent. And even if he went down to the basement's geothermal generators and set them to blow, that would only *increase* the level of security in the command centre. He needed fewer eyes on those computers, not more.

He rummaged through his bag. Nothing Sheni or Gecki owned was of any use in this situation, not even the plasma cutter. Alan flexed a pair of arms like dandelion stalks. There was nothing for it. He'd have to dispose of the guard himself.

Leaving his sack of goodies in the vent for safekeeping, he silently unscrewed the grate and dropped down onto the guard's terminal with all the rigidity of an arrow hitting a target. The guard stared at the smiling alien intruder in abject terror.

"What the—?"

Alan smacked the guard on top of the head with his wrench. He went down like a sack of freshly peeled spuds.

"You say something, Korri?"

Korri's co-worker looked over from their own computer just as Alan tugged the guard's unconscious body out of sight. After a moment's confusion they shrugged and got back to work.

"Must have gone on a bathroom break," they muttered.

Alan climbed onto Korri's seat and tapped away at the terminal. The other two officers were too engrossed in their own machines to notice him. He could navigate the operating system easily enough, but he couldn't find anything pertaining to his friends' particular cell. Nothing about the prison's directory made sense to him. It was all numbers, no names.

He hopped back down and inspected the wires and

tubes and poorly secured CPU casings on the underside of the desk. If he could just find the right component to break...

Alan swung his wrench into the computer as if he were using a machete to hack a path through dense jungle foliage. Sparks flew. Plastic cracked. The remaining two security officers rose from their respective terminals in open-mouthed horror.

"Who the—?" They hurriedly drew their sidearms. "What in the galaxy do you think you're doing?"

"Force quit," Alan giggled.

A klaxon like a foghorn with throat ache blasted from every speaker in the prison. Both security guards jerked their heads up as the lights of the Control Room suddenly flashed a mad and panicky red.

"Gods help us," the third officer said as they rushed back to watch the camera feeds.

Korri's colleague trained his handgun on Alan again, but the green menace was already gone.

CHAPTER SEVENTEEN

Sheni and Gecki were sitting in their cell on their respective bunks, fidgeting with their fingers and wondering why Alan was taking so long, when all hell broke loose in the prison. Klaxons wailed and warning lights flashed. The doors all rolled open. The drones monitoring the cell block tumbled past their catwalk and crashed into the concrete common area below.

"What the hell has that dribbling imbecile gone and done?" Gecki snarled.

"He's created the perfect distraction, that's what..."

Sheni approached the open door and watched through the bars as dozens of their incarcerated neighbours emerged from their cells, some less hesitantly than others. Their whoops and cheers could barely be heard over the sirens.

"*Is* it the perfect distraction, though?" Gecki grabbed Sheni's arm before he could leave the cell. "Every guard this side of Tübanc-Six is gonna be on the lookout for prisoners trying to escape. How are we supposed to sneak back to the ship now?"

"We improvise," Sheni said, clapping his hands together. "Come on!"

They sneaked out onto the catwalk running past their cell. As expected, the guards closest to the block came running at the first sign of commotion. Without the drones to back them up, they were hopelessly outnumbered. Sheni watched as one guard fired tranquilliser rounds into a pair of hoofed bovine inmates sprinting toward him, only for a Krolak prisoner to immediately barrel into him from behind. The four-armed reptilian picked the guard up and tossed him over the balcony.

"This way," Sheni said, quietly ushering Gecki in the opposite direction.

No sooner had they taken a step from their room than the canine Raklett came shuffling out of his own cell a few doors down. His fur was matted and rank, his jumpsuit in tatters, his eyes mad and bloodshot. There were holes in the rabid beast's deformed snout where gold rings used to be.

He turned to Sheni and grinned. Saliva splattered through the diamond-shaped latticework in the catwalk.

"Fresh meat," he growled.

The Raklett's look of psychopathic hunger turned to surprise as a dart struck his hairy shoulder. He glanced down at it, pulled it out – a spurt of blood splashed across what remained of his already bright red jumpsuit – and then took another step toward Sheni. Then three more darts shot into the psycho's flank and the Raklett dropped to the floor.

Sheni and Gecki ducked behind the wall of the catwalk as a guard stationed on the balcony opposite fired a dozen more tranquilliser darts, which clattered harmlessly against the concrete pillar behind them.

"Mangy dog like this ought to be put down for good,"

Gecki snarled as they scurried past the Raklett's sleeping body.

"You might be right," Sheni gasped, "but if we don't get out of this melee, we won't be getting up any time soon either. Do you remember the way back to the elevators? You know, the ones we rode with Captain Wrett?"

"Yeah, I reckon so. But don't forget, we've also got to find Alan before we leave."

"Don't worry. Knowing Alan, I'm sure he'll find us."

They sprinted off the catwalk and into the neighbouring corridor, the one down which they'd first been brought into the cell block. Nobody shot at them. The officer who'd tried to tranquillise them moments before now had other inmates to deal with. Sheni and Gecki planted themselves against the first wall they came across and cautiously peered around the corner.

A craggy inmate whose ancestor may well have been an alpine mountain was pummelling one of the masked guards into a paste with her fists. Sheni winced and looked the other way.

"You know, it won't be too long until they get all the security systems back online," Gecki rasped. "And fixing a prison break like this, they ain't always gonna be shooting to stun, you get me?"

"Yeah, I hear you. That's why we've got to get down to those administrative corridors, you know? The ones near the warden's tower. If everyone's busy containing the situation over here, that section of the prison should be fairly quiet, right?"

Gecki watched the adjacent corridor for an opening.

"You might have a point. And I s'pose we've gotta find an exit either way. Go."

They darted across to the next corridor. Sheni puffed out his cheeks, already out of breath.

"So, you still thinking we head back down through old Port Providence, pick up some more loot on the way?"

"Maybe." Gecki bared her teeth in irritation. "Would rather just waltz out the front door if we can. Or a back door, preferably. Don't fancy running into any more of those pirate ghouls if we can help it. But it depends on what's operational. Might not have a choice."

"I can see why you wanted to keep our escape quiet now," Sheni said, nodding. "Every cell and checkpoint *inside* the prison might be unlocked, but that doesn't mean the elevators and exterior doors haven't gone into full lockdown, right? Smart choice would be to keep them on altogether different systems, you know?"

"Exactly. But I guess we'll find out soon enough…"

They jumped as a panel in the corridor's ceiling gave way. Gecki brandished her claws. But it was only Alan who came crashing down the wall like an emerald bowling ball. He'd smeared streaks of dust and grease under his eyeballs like war paint.

"Look who it is," Gecki snarled. "*Someone's* been having fun, eh?"

A sack fell from the ceiling and landed in Alan's lap.

"Hey, he found our stuff!" Sheni rummaged through the bag for his clothes. "Good job, buddy."

He carefully checked behind the door of a nearby closet. It was empty save for tubs of bleach and detergent.

"Keep an eye out in case someone comes this way, will you? I'm gonna get changed."

"Is this really the time?" Gecki rasped.

"If it keeps me from sticking out like a freakin' overripe tomato, then yeah!"

Sheni switched his outfit while Gecki eagerly tore every scrap of jumpsuit from her body. Alan tied his now empty bag to the head of his wrench by its drawstrings so that it would billow out behind him like a flag.

Pocketing his data pad, Sheni re-emerged wearing his t-shirt, trousers and jacket, plus an over-confident smile on his face.

"Back to normality," he said as the tannoy speaker above their heads crackled and spiralled into a high-pitched death-whine. "Shall we?"

Gecki led the way, recalling the route they took the day before as best she could. It was hard when every corridor looked about as interesting as a pair of grey corduroy trousers, not to mention having to retrace their steps in reverse. Eventually they came to a stairwell. Sheni didn't remember a stairwell from his introduction to the prison facilities, but he *did* remember an elevator being involved, and considering the current state of the compound he reckoned one was about as good as the other.

They stumbled down five flights of steps. Just as they reached the bottom, a black-clad guard stepped out to block their path. Sheni was ninety percent convinced it was the same officer who taught him how to do his job in the workshop, and who hadn't been altogether comfortable with Sheni and Gecki being left alone with Captain Wrett afterwards, but the obsidian visor made it hard to tell for sure.

She nervously raised her rifle; he raised his hands. They stood like that for about five seconds while Gecki made a low growling sound deep in her throat before the officer sagged with exhaustion.

"Screw it," she said, jogging past them up the stairs. "The Ministry doesn't pay me enough for this."

Sheni and Gecki shrugged at each other and carried on.

The chaotic din of rifle fire and manic laughter and iron gates being slammed shut drifted down the stairwell behind them, but the corridors of the administrative wing were deserted. It was just as Sheni predicted. The Ministerium didn't have the budget to staff their prisons to begin with, especially those out in the middle of nowhere, let alone to cover every inch of the compound in the unlikely event of a full breakout. The riots were in and around the cell blocks, so that's where all the guards were, too.

They sprinted down the empty hallway, ignoring the frightened faces of admin workers peering out through the windows of their barricaded office doors, until they reached a fork in the corridor they recognised.

"This is it, right?" Sheni turned around slowly on the spot. "This is definitely where Captain Wrett brought us. Which means the warden's office is that way. Here, look. Says so on the sign."

"And the old cargo elevator leading down into Port Providence is *that* way, so..."

Sheni took a few slow steps backward in the direction of Warden Hills's tower. Gecki reared her head in frustration. Alan stood directly between them, smiling and waving his makeshift flag.

"Are you *seriously* still after that godsdamn sword?"

"I mean, if it's on the way, right?"

"How can it possibly be *on the way*, Sheni? The warden's office is up. The old outpost is down. They're as far apart as it gets!"

"Yeah, but, like, they're both in the same general vicinity, aren't they?"

"We're in the same general vicinity as them both *right now*, you idiot, but they are still very much in opposite directions. We get the sword *or* we escape the prison. Which one is it?"

Sheni clenched his jaw and balled his hands into fists, then let them fall to his sides.

"Look, Gecki. I know this scheme of mine went off the rails right from the start. I never should have drunkenly flown us halfway across the galaxy without your permission. Us getting thrown in jail? That's my fault, too. But we're so close, can't you see that?"

"Yeah. To the exit."

"You're not listening! That sword is worth millions of credits, Gecki, and it's *right there*. All we have to do is reach out and grab it. Don't you want to put an end to all this stealing and scrounging, you know, for good?"

Gecki sniffed and snorted and squinted down each of the corridors branching off from their crossroads. Finally she let out a hiss of resignation.

"Fine. Fine!" She pointed a scaly finger at Sheni's nose. "But only coz I figure there's gotta be a way out near the warden's tower anyway. If it's locked, or if I see so much as a single armed guard, we're going back the other way."

"Yes, Gecki! You know it's the right decision."

"I really freakin' don't."

They jogged down the corridor until they reached a security checkpoint. An Oortilian, much younger and paler than the warden with whom he shared a species, was the room's sole remaining staff member. A number-cruncher, judging by his simple, unpadded uniform. Sheni recognised him from their first trip to see Warden Hills. He let out a shriek as three intruders stormed into the room.

"Oh gods," he babbled, raising his hands. "Wait! I don't—"

"Sorry," Sheni said as he punched the Oortilian out cold. "No hard feelings, yeah?"

"What did I say about seeing any guards?" Gecki grumbled.

"That one doesn't count, surely?" he pleaded. "He didn't even have a gun."

The checkpoint was full of antiquated cabinets and computer equipment from the prison's original installation. Two lanes of yellow arrows were painted down the middle of the floor. A bulky security console on one side of the room stood next to a large pane of grease-smeared glass. Visible through it was another checkpoint, its mirror image, only this one appeared to be on the outside of the prison. If Sheni squinted hard he could make out rain sloshing down its windows.

Gecki crossed the room to where the corridor connecting the administrative wing to the warden's tower should have been. A steel shutter had slammed down in front of it.

"See, look." She tried to rattle the barrier, but it was too secure. "Emergency lockdown. Whole prison's gonna be like this. All except Port Providence."

"Yeah, well, we knew that was a possibility, didn't we?" Sheni fussed over the security console's numerous buttons and switches. "It's no biggie, right? Got the manual override lever right here. I'll just give it a tug…"

He pulled and he pulled, but it wouldn't shift an inch. He leaned over the console and peered through the bulletproof glass. Another identical lever was installed on the other side.

"Dammit!" Sheni pounded the console in frustration. "It's a dual-operator mechanism. We need someone in the other checkpoint to open it."

"Right, I said you had one shot and that was it." Gecki clicked her claws together as she marched back toward the corridor. "We're taking the elevator down to the outpost and sneaking back out the pipe like we should have done right from the start, got it?"

Sheni sighed.

"What if that's on lockdown, too?" he said, still leaning on the console. "Or the power could be out. And even if it isn't, we don't have all the biometric data we need to bypass its scanners."

"Then we'll find its maintenance hatch and climb down the shaft," Gecki replied, opening the door. "Down's down, right? Whatever we do, we can't stay…"

She took one look outside and immediately slammed it closed again.

"Quickly! Help me barricade the door!"

Sheni rushed over. A tide of red jumpsuits was rushing down the corridor toward them. Together they just about managed to tip a dusty relic of a filing cabinet over in front of the door before the horde could smash it off its hinges.

"Yeah," Sheni said through a grimace, "I don't think we're the only ones eager to pay the warden a visit…"

"That's the problem with you, though, isn't it? You *never* think!"

The filing cabinet shifted as the furious inmates continued to pound on the door. Sheni and Gecki put all of their weight against it as Alan hopped from workstation to workstation, presumably in search of something to eat.

"We have to get someone to pull the other lever," Sheni grunted.

"Yeah, and who's that gonna be? Prisoners can't get out there. Guards would rather see us die than let us through."

Glass got smashed on the other side of the door. They'd

taken out the lights. Sheni pulled the data pad from his jacket pocket.

"Only one person we can trust, right?"

"Ha! You know they won't do it. You'd have better luck asking the Ministry strike force when they get here."

"That's not fair, Gecki. Have a little faith, yeah?"

Sheni opened the pre-set comm channel with his back pushed up against the cabinet and his boots searching for grip on the frictionless floor. The call went through immediately.

"Hey, Xotl, it's Sheni. We need—"

"Sheni, is that you?" Xotl spluttered. "Thank the stars. Alan got hold of your data pad somehow and wasn't making the slightest bit of sense..."

"Xotl, stop talking for a second and listen. The warden caught us snooping about in Port Providence and threw us in prison. We're in the middle of breaking out but there's a lockdown in effect. We need you to come deactivate it from the other side."

An awkward pause.

"Xotl?" he asked, glancing at the screen to check the comm link hadn't been cut.

"You mean leave the ship," Xotl replied. "But Sheni, you know I can't do that. Imagine the foreign contaminants in a *prison* of all places..."

"Yeah, and normally I'd totally get that, you know, but—"

They ducked at the rattle of gunfire. It didn't sound very far away. Gecki grabbed the data pad from Sheni's hands.

"You listen to me, you flaccid echinoderm," she snarled. "I don't care how close you think you are to the grave – if you don't get your beaked arse over here pronto, the three of us are gonna beat you to it."

CHAPTER EIGHTEEN

Xotl rolled from arm to arm across the cockpit in anxious thought. If they'd had a heart, it would have been hammering. Their suckers tightened. They periodically pinned themselves to the floor they'd just spent half an hour waxing.

To venture outside meant risking illness, injury and death. But to remain on the ship surely secured the fate of every other member of the *Silver Hart's* crew. And without them, what was Xotl to do? Aimlessly sail the ship from star to star until their arms and disc became too calcified to operate the controls and then die alone?

"Oh, regrow a pair, Xotl," they spluttered. "The others wouldn't hesitate to risk their lives for you. Why should this be any different?"

Xotl flapped and flopped over to the cabinet in which the crew kept their various enviro-suits and pulled out the outfit Sheni and Gecki had commissioned for them. It was specially designed to accommodate a Xocha's physiology. Xotl had never worn it, not even to check if it fit. The Xocha weren't the type to wear clothes. Even wrapping a bandana around one of their arms was seen as a bit ostentatious. Besides, it was hard to find anything with the right number of sleeves.

They laid the enviro-suit on the floor, careful not to get any dust or dirt on the inside, and unsealed the two halves. One side was totally opaque, the other translucent, verging on transparent. If having a compromised immune system wasn't challenging enough, a Xocha's dozens of tiny eyes were scattered across all parts of their body. The entire suit needed to simultaneously operate as both armour and visor.

Xotl wriggled into position and threaded each of their arms down the 'gloves' at each end. Then they pulled the front-facing half back over themself. They didn't like this already. It was like climbing into one of those horrid human body bags.

Deep breaths through their beak. In and out. In and out.

They squeezed the button on the inside of their sleeve to seal themself in.

The squishy, gelatinous seam running the length of the suit closed together like a wound healing in fast-forward. The plastic tightened, shrank and expanded to fit Xotl's frame.

"Oh, this is quite horrible," they moaned. "I feel like a vacuum wrapped salmon."

Still, it was practically airtight. The only way for oxygen to get in or out was through a filter in the centre of the suit near Xotl's beak. It wasn't as thorough as the decontamination chamber installed in the ship's airlock, but it was a hundred times better than breathing in the planet's atmosphere without it. And the suit was surprisingly flexible, too. Xotl bent each of their arms in turn. A little rubbery, a little squeaky, but the Xocha weren't winning any marathons anyway. They just needed to remember that their suckers were out of action. No trying to climb up any walls today.

They went to descend the staircase, then hesitated. There could be all manner of threats out there. Prison guards. Fanged beasties. Especially sharp stones. One preserved starfish wasn't intimidating anybody. They cartwheeled further down the corridor to the cupboard in which they'd built their nest. They rarely used it these days, but old habits were hard to shake. Inside was a small taser for emergencies. Xotl strapped it to one of their arms using some of Alan's duct tape, then admired their handiwork.

"A spark glove," they spluttered. "At least I'm properly insulated, I suppose..."

They took each step down to the airlock delicately, the rubber tips of each arm providing limited grip compared to the suckers they were accustomed to, and pressed the button to open the interior set of doors. It had been a long time since they'd set foot – well, *ray* – inside the airlock. Years, in fact. The idea of leaving the comforting confines of the *Silver Hart* terrified Xotl more than Gecki could ever appreciate.

But it wasn't anywhere near as terrifying as the prospect of losing their friends forever.

Xotl rolled inside, punched the button and braced themself for an excruciatingly protracted death. The jets hissed, Xotl's suit misted up a little, and then the exterior set of doors whooshed open.

There it was: the world outside, and the galaxy beyond. Xotl tensed and trembled, but they guessed they weren't dead yet. A good start by any yardstick. Of course, it could take days before the bacteria in the air began the process of breaking down their skin gills...

Steps clattered down from the airlock to the rocky canyon floor. Xotl slowly followed them down, one at a time. They were still on the ship, technically speaking. On it, just outside of it. Each small step both literal and figurative. The drizzle left streaky raindrops on the front of their semi-transparent suit.

Xotl reached the bottom and stretched out an arm. They prodded the stones with its tip. There. Done it. No big deal. Nothing scary about a bunch of old, damp stones.

Yet they remained standing there on the bottom step as if the calcification had already taken root.

Stop it, Xotl. You're better than this. You used to love the outdoors, growing up on Estroidea. Sunshine on the shore, remember? This is exactly the same, only this time you're tucked up safe in a suit.

Xotl put one arm on the rocks. Then another so that they were standing upright with their remaining three arms held out for balance. They uncoiled the tip of one arm from the metal steps. Nothing tethering them to the ship now. They reached out in the opposite direction, adjusting their body so that they switched from arm to arm in a clockwise motion, turning like the spokes of a wheel, gradually at first, and then faster.

They were on the move.

Xotl couldn't smile, what with having the rigid beak of an octopus, but inside they were wearing a goofier grin than even Alan could hope to achieve.

I am Xotl. I am a vital member of this crew.
And I am not afraid.

But the water in their vascular system turned ice cold when they stopped to look back at the ship. They'd barely gone more than ten metres. Sheni, Gecki and Alan were under siege. They could die at the hands of blood-crazed prisoners at any moment. It might already be too late.

"I have to be quicker," they spluttered as they cartwheeled on. "Hold tight, everyone. I'm on my way."

Up over the rocks they gyrated in arhythmic flapping movements. Over the pebbles and plains they cartwheeled. The suit was more resilient than Xotl had given it credit for. No breaches in the plastic yet, despite one precarious tumble. The semi-transparent front was getting splattered with muck and rain, though, and it was getting harder to see. Perhaps Sheni could wipe it down with a microfibre cloth once they were reunited.

They paused for the skin gills around their beak to collect oxygen. Fresh air. Even though it was being filtered by the suit, this was probably the least recycled atmosphere they'd breathed in years. It was a shame that the filters sucked all the smell out of it.

The prison stood at the top of the cliff. A solid block of unnatural grey concrete flanked by castle towers. Lightning crackled in the distance. From outside, nothing looked amiss. There was no clue as to the chaos ravaging it from within.

Sheni had said they were trapped in a security checkpoint close to the tallest of the four towers, that a similar checkpoint lay on the outside of the facility. Xotl thought they saw the squat building in question, but it could have been just another smudge on their full-body visor, and trying to wipe their suit clear of muck only seemed to make it worse.

They steeled themself and rolled on. Hopefully the

others could keep the lunatics in the asylum at bay a little while longer.

Not far now.

Officer Helio stood trembling in the rain.

Backup was coming. The various internal security and communication systems of the T-6 Correctional Facility may have been down, but the comm link in his personal data pad wasn't. He'd made the call. Help was on its way.

He just had to hold his nerve and stay put until the Ministry cruiser got here. Their strike teams would handle the rest.

Whether any of his colleagues would still have their jobs when all this was over – or their lives, he added with a shiver – was another thing entirely. Right at that moment, Helio thought being stationed anywhere other than this sorry sodden rock sounded pretty godsdamn good, actually.

He lingered anxiously outside the checkpoint with his back to the prison and his eyes on the stormy skyline. There were inmates on the other side of the glass. Or at least he thought they were inmates. They weren't wearing the usual red jumpsuits. Regardless, he'd chosen to ignore them. Like hell was he going to be the officer responsible for letting a horde of degenerates run amok over the planet.

"Excuse me," said a clacking, warbling voice to his right. "Is this the security checkpoint providing access to the warden's tower?"

Helio slowly turned his numb neck. A five foot purple starfish wrapped in a cellophane mackintosh was standing politely next to him. For all he'd been terrified of the reprobates on the other side of the prison's walls, he hadn't considered that somebody dangerous might still be crazy enough to try and get in. He broke from his stupor and scrambled to unholster his sidearm.

"What the—"

"I am dreadfully sorry," the starfish spluttered, prodding him with one of their plastic-wrapped arms.

Helio's spine arched as a thousand volts of electricity pulsed through his body, then he went sprawling into the mud where he quickly began snoring.

Xotl kept their spark glove held aloft as they waddled past Helio into the exterior checkpoint. The rest of the small, sparse room was deserted, though its scanners and security belts still blinked and bleeped within its otherwise lifeless concrete walls. Whether the other guards had rushed inside when the riot broke out or there'd only been the one guard stationed there to begin with, Xotl couldn't tell, but they sure were glad not to have to zap anyone else. It wasn't exactly how they'd imagined reintegrating themself with society.

There was a semi-enclosed corridor leading from the checkpoint to the prison's entrance foyer. A sign had been installed above its dull, metal archway. *Tübanc-Six Correctional Facility*, it read in stocky, no-nonsense runes. An industrial security shutter had closed over it. Beside this was a security console, behind which ran a long, grubby window.

Alan was standing behind the glass, dribbling and banging the pane with his wrench.

"Alan!" Xotl rolled towards the window. "Thank goodness you are still alive. Are Gecki and Sheni with you, too?"

Sheni's tired and sweaty face appeared at the window behind Alan. He broke into an enormous grin and shouted something to a third person Xotl couldn't see. Gecki, they presumed. They couldn't hear a word Sheni said, though.

He crossed to the security console on his side and pressed a button. The speakers on Xotl's side crackled on with a pathetic whine.

"Xotl, you absolute hero. Hey, Gecki. Look who showed up!"

"Yes, yes, well done Xotl," Gecki snarled from the other side of the room. "Can we get rid of that freakin' shutter already?"

"Oh, yeah." Sheni grabbed hold of the lever on his side. "On the count of three, I need you to pull that lever down, all right? Okay? One, two, *three*..."

Xotl wrapped an arm around the lever on their side and pulled hard. It resisted at first, then slammed down with a solid *thunk*. The shutters on both Xotl and Sheni's sides of the glass rolled up into their respective ceilings.

"It's open," Sheni yelled, "go!"

Gecki sprinted from her spot reinforcing the barricade at the door. Sheni tossed Alan to her as she passed. Xotl watched as the door behind them shook and buckled and bent.

"I'll find you inside," the starfish spluttered, pointing an arm toward the corridor that led to the foyer. "With any luck we'll meet up in the middle."

Sheni shot Xotl a thumbs-up and then sprinted off after Gecki and Alan. Xotl watched the door shake and the filing cabinet shift a few more inches across the security room floor before they rolled hesitantly down the external corridor. It sounded like a pack of wild animals had broken loose in there.

"In for a penny," they muttered as they passed from arm to arm. "In for a pound..."

CHAPTER NINETEEN

Sheni and Gecki sprinted away from the checkpoint until they reached another door leading outside. Rain dripped off a concrete awning. This door they barricaded, too.

"Stars above," Sheni gasped, piling up another wooden pallet. "Why do they have to make finding one's way out of a prison so damn complicated?"

"Yeah, it's one of life's great mysteries," Gecki snarled. "We should have headed underground when we had the chance."

"But then we wouldn't be anywhere near as close to becoming millionaires." Sheni pointed to the entrance of the warden's tower just a short walk away. "And Xotl's already secured our way out through the foyer, basically. All things considered, it's all going to plan, you know?"

Gecki smacked Sheni around the back of the head.

"Everything goes to plan when your plan is to improvise, you dolt!"

"Extemporary exertion," Alan gurgled.

"Hey, it looks like we're in the strip between the prison

yard and the outer wall." Sheni winced as he rubbed the back of his skull. "We're definitely headed in the right direction. Only guards and guests are supposed to get in here."

"Yeah, but we ain't past the scopes of the snipers up in the watch towers yet," Gecki rasped. "So what d'ya say we stop standing here yapping and get on with stealing that sword before someone blows your head off?"

"It feels like someone already has…"

They ran down the strip of no-man's land together before the barricaded door behind them could start quaking and shaking again. Past the hulking mass of the primary prison building, the yard came fully into view. It was a war zone drenched in blood and spotlights. Battered and bruised officers had retreated to the outdoors and were making a last stand against the advancing inmates, presumably hoping that their colleagues in the watch towers could help even the odds. Sheni wasn't sure whether their plan was working or not. Bodies in uniforms and jumpsuits alike littered the barren concrete.

He ducked at the sound of assault rifles being fired. Sheni was no expert on firearms and munitions, but something told him the guards weren't using tranquillisers anymore.

"Careful." Gecki pulled him against the exterior wall, and Sheni did the same to Alan. "Eyes in the sky."

One of the watch towers' searchlights swept back and forth along the barbed wire fence. The three of them were just about hidden by the bulging girth of the warden's tower and the stacks of delivery pallets left to rot in the rain.

"Who they're searching for, I don't know," Gecki rasped irritably. "All the fighting's going on right there."

"And the door to Warden Hills's office is right *there*."

Sheni nodded to the entrance only half a dozen metres further on. "Let's just make a run for it. They won't see us."

"Patience, you idiot. Unless that warden's got a set of thrusters built into the base of his tower, he's not going anywhere."

Sheni squinted through the drizzle and barked out a mirthless laugh.

"Hey, look at that. Seems like good old Captain Wrett is getting a taste of her own medicine."

The power-armoured Drygg was backing away from a trio of inmates. The first of them took a running leap at her. Captain Wrett cracked their skull with her electric baton. Then the others pounced and pinned her to the floor, bludgeoning the captain with their calloused claws and fists. Sheni winced.

"You know, I think our little uprising *might've* gotten out of hand," he said, glancing back the way they came. "If we don't get to the warden soon, there won't be much of a warden left!"

"All right, all right. Searchlight's gone, anyway."

Sheni darted to the door, but it was flung open before he could even reach for the handle. A boot kicked Sheni in the chest and he flew backward onto the unforgiving concrete.

Iskar Barabba staggered through the doorway, his jumpsuit ripped and covered in blood.

"You bunch of deceitful bilge rats," he spat. "That demented pet of yours owes me a godsdamn tooth!"

"Let it go, you daft Kerulian," Gecki rasped as Sheni picked himself back up. "Stop whining and walk out the godsdamn door."

"You really still think we abandoned you?" Sheni added. "We've got a ship waiting to get us off this planet. Consider yourself rescued!"

"I'm not going anywhere without my brother," Iskar grunted. "Thanks for the heads up about the ship, though. We'll make good use of it."

He pulled out a shiv fashioned from a spoon stolen from his cell block's canteen. Sheni raised his hands.

"Don't be hasty, Iskar. Think of the credits we owe you..."

The Kerulian only managed a single step out of the doorway before he jerked in agony and collapsed to the ground. Sheni laughed in relief. Xotl stood behind Iskar in the base of the tower with their taser still spitting out sparks.

"I never thought I'd have my skin saved by a five-armed prophylactic." Sheni fist-bumped one of Xotl's plastic limbs. "Good to see you, Xotl. How's life outside the ship treating you?"

"I have already rendered four individuals unconscious," Xotl replied matter-of-factly. "No, five. I must admit I'm finding all of this rather exhilarating."

"Yes, well, fun as this all is," Gecki snarled, "I rather think we've outstayed our welcome. Exit's through there, is it?"

"Indeed. Through the welcome foyer and down the external security corridor, and then it's a quick roll back down the hill to the *Silver Hart*."

"Great work. Lead the way."

"Woah, hold on." Sheni grabbed Gecki's scaly arm. "Aren't you forgetting something? What about the sword?"

"Screw it," she snarled. "Like you said, this place is gonna be overrun by inmates at any moment."

"The Sword of Bokata?" Xotl's arms went rigid with surprise. "You actually found it?"

"Yeah, but the warden confiscated it before he threw us in a cell. It's sitting in his office right above our heads!"

"Then surely we must retrieve it first," Xotl said, turning to Gecki. "Is that not the reason we came out here?"

"Just coz it's the reason for coming here," Gecki snarled, "doesn't make it a reason to stay."

"I dare say that if you heard about a priceless relic going ignored during a prison break," Xotl spluttered, "you'd be the first to suggest we sneak in and grab it while nobody's watching. And discovering the Sword of Bokata *was* my special request, if you recall. One last big score for old times' sake. But, of course, *you* are the captain. It has to be your decision."

Gecki sneered at the three expectant faces watching her. Well. One expectant face, another gormless one, and a particularly mutinous beak. Gods. Their camaraderie was almost nauseating.

"Fine, but make it freakin' quick!"

Sheni clapped his hands together in triumph and rushed to the elevator up which he'd been shepherded the day before. He tapped the button on the scanner but nothing happened. Just a dull click. The lockdown, of course. By the time Sheni figured it out, the rest of his crew were already halfway up the first flight of stairs.

He considered how tall the warden's tower was, how tired his legs were, and then cracked his neck from side to side. If even Xotl could get up there...

"One small step for a man," he muttered as he chased after them. "One giant leap for an agoraphobic starfish..."

CHAPTER TWENTY

The doors to Warden Hills's office burst open. The lone officer stationed outside came soaring through, out cold with a broken nose.

Sheni, Gecki, Alan and Xotl marched in as one, their fists and tentacle-arms clenched.

"That sword," Sheni said, jabbing a finger at the warden, "belongs to us."

Warden Hills stumbled backward from the door in spluttering indignation. Clearly he hadn't expected any of the inmates to get this far. They'd never had a prisoner successfully escape before, and now all of them were breaking out at once.

"You," the Oortilian said as he bumped into his desk. "You can't be in here! I'll see you hang for this, you lousy pond scum!"

"That sort of talk doesn't sound very Ministerial," Gecki snarled. "Hand over the godsdamn sword and we'll all be on our way, got it?"

"Wait, who or what is *that?*" Warden Hills pointed a trembling blue finger at Alan, who smiled back with all the density of a neutron star. "Hold on. That's the *thing* the officers in the Control Room told me about. This is all you, isn't it? This madness is all *your* doing."

Outside the tower's windows, down in the prison yard below, something exploded in a miniature mushroom cloud of green-blue flames. Inmates and officers continued to shoot and bludgeon one another. Some of the wire fences had been torn down.

"All of this," Hills screeched, "just for one old blade?"

"It's a bit much, I will admit," Sheni said, shrugging apologetically. "But you didn't *have* to steal our stuff and throw us in a cell, you know."

"You broke into Ministry property!"

"Nah." Gecki glared at the warden with her one good eye. "We broke into pirate property which *your* Ministry stole."

"This all boils down to a difference of perspective," Xotl spluttered, sparking their taser-glove. "How about we take that sword off your hands, Mr. Warden, and leave you here to piece your prison back together unharmed?"

Warden Hills stared at Xotl as if only noticing them for the first time.

"And who are you, exactly?" he babbled. "We don't even house your kind here..."

The Sword of Bokata still rested on Hills's desk. Its bronze handle was considerably more shiny than the tarnished blade. Sheni saw an opening and darted forward to grab it. He wrapped a hand around its raggedy hilt before the warden even had time to turn around.

"Escape the prison if you must," Hills pleaded. "I can have the records scrubbed. It'll be like you were never here. But leave me the sword. Do you know how many years I've slaved away in this pig pen? That blade's my retirement!"

"And do you have any idea how long we've fought tooth and claw to get by, constantly struggling to get out from under the thumb of people like you?" Sheni backed away slowly, the sword raised. "Nah, man. Sorry. Finders keepers. Leave this tower and discover your own ancient relic, you want one so badly."

Everybody jumped as a stream of bullets sprayed across the tower's windows. The glass cracked where each round hit, but none of the panes shattered. A prisoner had found their way around the biometric locks installed on the guards' assault rifles, it seemed. Either that, or even the officers had had enough.

"We've got the sword," Gecki rasped. "Now let's go!"

They turned and hurried back to the tower's stairwell as fast as they could with a cellophane-wrapped starfish in tow. Sheni heard Hills scrabbling about under the desk behind them. When he glanced over his shoulder, the warden was upright again and pointing a handgun at them. Its ceremonial wooden box, a privilege of the warden's rank, lay open on the desk.

"Stop!" Hills cried out. "Come back this instant! You are inmates of the T-6 Correctional Facility, and... and you other two are aiding in their escape! You are all under arrest. Again. Now put down that sword and surrender yourselves peacefully or I *will* shoot you!"

Sheni glanced at Gecki, who bared her teeth, and then walked back into the warden's office with the sword held out wide. The rest of the crew followed behind him, slowly.

"Come on, man. There's no need for things to turn violent, you know? Put the gun down. There's four of us and one of you. If you pull that trigger, things ain't gonna go well for any of us, you hear me?"

"You don't think I'll shoot?" Warden Hills trembled his

way around to the front of his desk again. "Is that it? Because as warden, I'm perfectly within my rights."

"To shoot inmates?" Gecki rasped.

"To defend myself against them! Against you! Look at the way this one's coming at me..."

"Hurting you is the last thing I want." Sheni made a show of gradually setting the sword down on the floor. "What I *want* is for you to hand me the gun and then take a seat while the rest of us get the hell out of here..."

Warden Hills only tightened his shaky grip on his handgun. Gecki extended her claws. Xotl stepped closer with their taser primed. Alan raised his wrench. Hills pointed the gun at each one of them in turn, growing more panicky with each twitch.

"Sheni," Gecki rasped cautiously, "I don't think this guy's gonna listen to reason..."

"Stay back," Hills yelled. "Put your weapons down and, and... and lie there until the Ministry cruiser gets here!"

"Don't do anything stupid, Warden," Sheni said, the tip of the sword almost touching the floor now, his other hand stretched out for Hills's gun. "Take your own advice and—"

"I said *stay back!*"

Whether or not Warden Hills intended to pull the trigger wasn't clear – the Oortilian was shaking too hard to even hold the handgun properly. But either way, the gun went off. Sheni felt something barrel into his side at the last second and went crashing onto the floor, sword still in hand. He didn't feel any pain besides a slightly bruised rib. Maybe the bullet had passed right through his spinal column and left him totally numb.

But that couldn't be true. He was already kneeling up. He could feel the cold metal handle of the sword in his clenched fist and the ache in his side where something distinctly un-bullet-like had thumped into him. And his motor skills appeared fine, because he was rising to his feet and swinging the Sword of Bokata toward Warden Hills quite without intending to do so.

Its sickly-green blade sliced a thin, red gash across the back of Hills's hand. The warden dropped the gun and stumbled backward into one of the chairs beside his desk, cursing and clutching at his bloody knuckles.

Gecki stomped toward him, claws raised and teeth ready to shred flesh from bone.

"It's okay," Sheni called out. "He missed."

"No, he didn't," she snarled back, spittle flying.

Sheni spun around. Xotl was on their back, arms splayed and pointing up at the ceiling. Their beak clacked wordlessly. Though still smiling, Alan was fretting beside the Xocha, hopping from foot to foot and patting the starfish reassuringly.

Sheni dropped to his knees beside Xotl and searched for an entry wound.

"You're not bleeding," he said. "That's good, right?"

"Xocha don't have blood," Xotl replied. Their voice sounded even wetter than usual. "Water carries oxygen and nutrients around our bodies, so we... *hngnh*..."

Sheni found a puncture mark in the suit. There was a hole in Xotl's disc right between the third and fourth arms. He ran a hand around it. Sure enough, both the inside and outside of Xotl's enviro-suit were extremely damp.

"Okay, don't talk. It's gonna be okay, you know? We'll find someone who can patch you up. Maybe the prison doctor can help."

"They will not understand my physiology. As the warden said, they don't house my kind here. And that's presuming, of course, that the doctor isn't dead."

Gecki continued to stalk murderously toward Warden Hills. But she stopped short when she heard him muttering and growling to himself. His wounded hand hung limp by his side and dripped blood onto the floor.

"Erm, Sheni?" she rasped, reversing direction. "Does something about the warden seem, you know, kinda familiar to you?"

"Yeah, course it does," Sheni replied, irritated with his reptilian captain for not treating Xotl's injury seriously enough. "We've been chatting with him for minutes now and we met him only…"

Warden Hills raised his head. His eyes were glassy and bloodshot, the sockets dark and sunken. His skin was turning a veiny sort of grey-green colour. From the way his jaw hung in a hungry yawn and he kept twitching his head from left to right like an animal defending its territory, the warden had transformed from a prim coward to a feral beast.

Just like the pirates down in Port Providence, only with about eight decades' less decay.

"…yesterday. Ah. Yeah, I see what you mean."

"It's that freakin' sword, Sheni. You were right. One nick from that blade and you turn into a godsdamn monster!"

Hills suddenly leapt at her, snarling and snapping his jaw. Gecki grabbed the warden around the throat and squeezed tight. The skin on his neck tore and bled, his larynx cracked, but the madman just kept coming. She kept him at arm's length and jerked her head back to dodge his slashing hands. She was lucky Oortilians didn't have fingernails.

"A little help here?" she snarled.

"Help? What do you expect *me* to do?"

"Shoot him or stab him, just do something!"

Stabbing the warden had caused this mess, so Sheni elected to go with the gun. Scrambling across to where it had clattered onto the floor, he aimed the handgun at its deranged owner's head. But Hills was moving about too much, and Sheni had never been all that great a shot.

"It's no use," he shouted, lowering the gun. "I'm more likely to hit you!"

"For the love of..." She hissed through her flared nostrils. "Fine, I'll take care of it myself."

Gecki charged across the office with the warden still clutched in her powerful claws. She stopped just short of one of the windows already fractured by stray bullets and flung him through it. The glass erupted outwards and Warden Hills fell from the tower still shrieking and trying to hack at her. A wet thud as flesh met rock. Gecki turned back to Sheni with a cold, faraway look in her eye.

"Okay. Now we've *really* gotta go."

She stomped across the floor and carefully scooped Xotl up in her arms. The starfish had lost consciousness. Sheni and Alan chased after her.

"Don't forget the sword, you idiot!" she rasped back at him.

"Really?" Sheni replied as he went back to snatch the blade off the floor. "How is *that* of any concern right now?"

"Because if Xotl dies, all this had better not be for nothing!"

CHAPTER TWENTY-ONE

Xotl was heavier than they looked, but Gecki had little trouble lugging them down the hundred-odd steps of the tower. Sheni panted and coughed behind her, Sword of Bokata in hand. It was only when he reached the bottom that he realised he still had Warden Hills's handgun clutched in the other.

"Keep the pointy end of that thing away from me," Gecki snarled when he almost barrelled into her from behind. "I ain't turning out like our warden friend. First thing we're doing once we're outta here is finding that sword a gods-damn sheath."

"Well, not the first thing," Sheni gasped, nodding at Xotl. "How are they doing?"

"Not great. Xotl's out cold and losing a lot of fluid. We need to think of someone who can fix them up."

Gecki marched toward the prison's welcome foyer. Sheni lingered in the base of the warden's tower a little longer. Iskar Barabba's unconscious body was just about visible through the open door.

"What are you doing, human? Hurry up!"

"Shouldn't we, you know, drag him out of the prison with us?"

"What? No! The guy's an arsehole, Sheni. He tried to kill us. Twice. Leave him here to rot."

"But we did just hide while he got captured, Gecki. It was *kind* of our fault."

"No, it wasn't. We all knew the risks and we all had our part to play. It was never the plan for Iskar to get caught. Things just don't always turn out okay for everyone. He's only blaming us to avoid blaming himself. Now, are you coming or not?"

She stomped off. Alan pottered after her, occasionally jumping up to pat one of Xotl's drooping arms. Sheni hesitated, then squatted down beside Iskar and shrugged.

"Sorry, man. You tried to kill us because you thought we betrayed you and left you for dead. We didn't. But you *did* try and kill us, so I guess leaving you behind now kind of makes us even, yeah?"

He weighed up the warden's gun in his hand. In lieu of a set of skeleton keys, it was about as good a ticket out of the prison as any. Presuming Iskar didn't wake up before the Ministry reinforcements got here, of course.

But then again, Iskar wasn't going to leave without his brother, Javik. Which meant that giving him a weapon would put a lot more inmates and officers at risk. And spacers weren't exactly known for their forgive and forget philosophy. If Iskar did decide to come after the crew of the *Silver Hart* looking for revenge, the last thing Sheni wanted was to give him the means to exact it.

Plus, a ceremonial weapon gifted to those who rose up through the ranks of prison officers had to be worth a credit or two, right?

"I'd wish you good luck, but..." He stood up and

stuffed the gun into the waistband of his trousers. "Maybe you and your brother should treat this place as an opportunity to take a long, hard look at your attitude to life, yeah?"

Sheni jogged down the corridor into the foyer. Though it matched the rest of the facility's Brutalist design, the foyer was much nicer – pillars that were polished and dusted, cushioned seating, holographic posters selling the merits of rehabilitation. Gecki and Alan were already gone. Fortunately, the guards Xotl had knocked out on their way in – plus one unfortunate prisoner who'd come so close to escape – were still unconscious. Sheni hurried past them toward the exterior security checkpoint. Another officer, snoring peacefully. He glanced back through the glass into the other security checkpoint, the mirrored one in which he and Gecki had been trapped, and witnessed numerous inmates smashing up all the terminals. Good luck getting *that* lockdown back in place.

He caught up with Gecki just a few dozen metres down the rocky slope. Rain was pitter-pattering against Xotl's plastic enviro-suit. Water was surely getting inside the outfit, but Sheni wondered if it was the right *kind* of water. Or what damage the planet's unfiltered atmosphere was doing to Xotl's nervous system.

"Good choice," Gecki rasped. "That sorry Kerulian wouldn't move a muscle to save you if the roles were reversed. In fact, he'd probably slit your throat while you slept."

"Yeah, well. There's a good reason why most of these inmates are behind bars. After all the commotion we've caused, I figure we don't need to be setting any of them free. Besides us, of course."

"Of course. You thought of a doctor yet?"

Sheni wracked his brains as they skidded through the gravelly grit past the sewer entrance to Port Providence.

"What about Skratchitt at the Corpse & Casket? Cheap rates. Always done a good job of patching us up."

"You kidding? Guy's a hack. And cheap ain't exactly my priority right now."

"Yeah, but we're not exactly rolling in credits, are we? Fine, what about Estroidea then? Best place to treat a Xocha has gotta be their homeworld, right?"

"You'd think so," Gecki snarled. "But you know how reclusive their type normally is. No way are they letting our grubby ship into their atmosphere, not without a month's worth of paperwork and red tape. And even if they did, they ain't gonna treat Xotl. Dumb starfish isn't even allowed back on the planet."

They clambered over the shale boulders, slipping in the worsening rain. Sheni was soaked through. Gecki had to pass Xotl over to him on a couple of occasions so that she could scale the rocks unhindered. Alan hopped about anxiously.

"Kapamentis, then?" Sheni suggested, passing Xotl back to Gecki. "The hospitals there specialise in all sorts of species."

"Might have to be. We'll take out a loan if we need to. Find some way to pay the surgeon back. Done it before, we'll do it again. You got any connections there who can help?"

"Yeah, I dunno... maybe a friend of a friend..."

They sprinted the rest of the distance to the ship. Gecki hissed in frustration as the airlock insisted on performing its usual decontamination cycle. They hastily dragged Xotl up into the cockpit. It felt wrong to leave them anywhere else.

"Fill up a bucket with water, Alan," Gecki commanded. "We need to keep Xotl hydrated."

Alan dropped his wrench and waddled off in the direction of the galley. Sheni knelt down and brought his ear close to Xotl's beak and skin-gills.

"I don't think they're breathing," he said, eyes wide with alarm.

"Peel them out of that godsdamn suit," Gecki snarled as she climbed into the pilot's seat.

Sheni fumbled with the enviro-suit in search of the nub the shopkeeper had told him about back when they bought it. He found it between two of the arms. He squeezed and twisted the nub clockwise and the seal came unstuck. He threw off the top half of the suit and once more checked if the starfish was still alive.

"Breathing's faint, but it's there," Sheni said, nodding erratically. "I don't know how much longer they can hold on, though."

"It's just a few hours to Kapamentis," Gecki rasped as she ignited the *Silver Hart's* thrusters. "Keep fighting, Xotl. You might be dying, but you ain't dying *yet*."

CHAPTER
TWENTY-TWO

Sheni paced back and forth along the stark grey corridor, scratching at the back of his neck and muttering to himself. Gecki lurked nearby, leaning against a concrete wall and picking at the strips of meat stuck between her teeth. Alan dribbled.

Xotl had stopped breathing before they could bring them to someone who could help. Only for a few minutes, but still.

The doctors were doing everything they could, but all the rest of the crew could do was wait.

And wait.

And wait…

The three of them stood around Xotl's glass-lidded hyperbaric chamber wearing gloomy expressions. The doctors had all left about ten minutes earlier.

"There's no hope for it," Gecki rasped. "It's a goner. Have to toss it out the airlock."

"No need to litter the galaxy," Sheni replied. "Just dump it in a skip somewhere."

"I'm not dead," Xotl spluttered.

"Oh, what?" Sheni replied, cracking a mischievous smile. "We were, erm... we were talking about your enviro-suit."

"Yeah," Gecki added. "Apparently it won't work so good with a great big hole in it. Who knew?"

"How are you feeling, buddy?" Sheni asked.

"Rather numb," Xotl replied. "I suspect this is a good thing. Repairing Xocha tissue can be a particularly itchy process. It's not easy to scratch with suckers, let me tell you. What's the diagnosis?"

"Full recovery," Gecki replied, grinning. "The doctors left it to us to deliver the good news."

"They confirmed your, you know, *pre-existing condition*," Sheni said with a shrug. "Reckon you've got years left in you, though. Other than that, the gunshot wound should heal up nicely on its own and you'll be cleared in a day or two. You were clinically dead for a little while, but there's no keeping a good starfish down for long, right?"

"And any infections?" Xotl asked anxiously.

"Streptococcus pneumoniae," Alan gurgled happily.

"You caught a bacteria that caused a mild fever," Sheni explained. "Nothing a course of antibiotics won't fix. You're already pumped full of them."

Xotl deflated in their padded chamber.

"That is a relief. Wait a moment." They jerked as upright as the intravenous drips running into their arms would allow. "Where in the galaxy are we? We can't afford this kind of treatment."

"No, we can't." Gecki shrugged. "So it's a good thing we ain't paying for it."

"Oh no," Xotl spluttered. "What have you done...?"

"Nothing," Sheni said, laughing. "Don't get your suckers in a twist. Remember Jack Bishop, that human we ran into during the Copperhead days? I called him on the way here—"

"Where *is* here, for that matter?"

"Oh, yeah. Kapamentis. So, I told Jack it was an emergency and needed a favour. Matter of actual life and death. Turns out that Krettelian friend of his works at the Ministry now. She pulled a few strings. Had to tell the staff we were war heroes of the Battle for Kapamentis, though."

"Which we *are*," Gecki said, jabbing a claw at Sheni's chest.

"Hold on, so that means..."

"We're in the medical wing of the Ministerium headquarters," Gecki rasped, nodding. "Kind of ironic after everything that went down in the prison, ain't it?"

"Keep your voice down," Sheni whispered. "I'd hardly put it past the Ministry to plant bugs in their treatment rooms!"

Gecki rolled her one good eye.

"What they gonna do, put us on trial for leaving a prison we were never legally put in to begin with? The extranet news networks would have a field day. Besides, I don't reckon Hills ever actually got round to adding us to the system. Would have raised a lot of questions with his superiors back here, don't you think?"

"Yeah, I guess..."

"Plus," Gecki added loudly for the benefit of any microphones listening, "I heard the prison break was all that Iskar Barabba's doing."

Sheni elbowed her in the ribs and then leaned against the transparent lid of Xotl's chamber.

"We've put in an order for a new enviro-suit, by the way. We'll need one to get you from here to the *Silver Hart*. It should be ready by the time the doctors release you. Not that I expect you'll be wanting to use it much, you know, after everything that happened."

"Quite the contrary," Xotl spluttered. "I haven't had that much fun in cycles. Leaving the confines of the ship was rather exhilarating up until the suit and I were perforated. A replacement would be much appreciated, presuming we can afford to spend the credits. Though I dare say I will be sticking to less hostile environments in future."

"Agreed," Gecki rasped. "Those enviro-suits ain't exactly armoured, and you are a rather squishy species. Let's hope we can all avoid getting caught up in any more prison breaks for a while, yeah?"

"Hey, Xotl." Sheni rapped his knuckles on the chamber's lid. "We made it out of there with the Sword of Bokata, by the way. Never would have discovered it if it hadn't been for you."

"That's wonderful news. Have you found a buyer already?"

"Not yet. We figured we'd go through Peggi Slim at the Corpse & Casket, but then we remembered – the sword isn't stolen. No need to go through a fence! And there are loads of private collectors and museum curators right here on Kapamentis. There's actually an auction tonight. We're gonna submit it, provided the Ministry gives it back in time for the authentication process."

"They wanted to keep hold of it permanently, on account of it being a deadly weapon," Gecki snarled, "till I reminded them the same thing can be said of any regular blade, too."

"They did print a plastic sheath for it, though," Sheni added, "so no-one's gonna accidentally prick themselves and end up like the warden."

"Which of course we don't know anything about," Gecki said to the hidden microphones, "because we were never there."

"Why does the Ministerium even have it?" Xotl asked.

"We had to set the *Silver Hart* down in the loading bay out the back of the headquarters," Sheni explained, scratching his neck. "It was the only way to get you close enough to the medical wing for transportation. And like hell were we paying Kapamentis parking charges, you know? But that meant they had to inspect the ship. Standard protocol. And a weird sword is exactly the sort of thing those jackbooted grunts *love* to confiscate."

"Fascists," Alan cooed.

"There's a silver lining, though," Sheni continued. "When they ran the sword through all their scanners and tests and stuff, the geeks in the lab figured out why it made the warden and the old pirates go so crazy."

"Yeah," Gecki snarled. "And it ain't magic, just like I said it wouldn't be."

"The blade's infested with some kind of fungus. When it cuts you, it gets in your blood and then your brain, and after that you lose all cognitive and motor functions. Even after the host's body technically dies, the fungus lives on in their nervous system. I'm guessing it put what remained of Flinthawk's old pirate crew into a sort of dormant state down in Port Providence's catacombs once it ran out of people to infect."

"Easy to bide your time when you're a mushroom," Gecki added, crossing her arms.

Xotl's tentacle-arms wilted slightly. They were growing tired.

"So when the legends said that Bokata could make his enemies bend the knee simply by being in possession of the sword...?"

"Only half true, I guess." Sheni shrugged. "I figure they bowed down and followed him, all right. He just slaughtered them first."

"Bokata might have possessed the sword," Gecki mused, "but in a way, the sword kinda possessed them..."

"Goodness." Xotl sank back down onto their padded bedding. "Well, I shall be glad to have it off my ship, then. What time is this auction?"

"Five hours from now." Sheni checked the clock on his data pad. "Speaking of which, we ought to get a move on if we want to retrieve the sword from those boffins and register it in time to make the catalogue..."

"Go on, have fun." Xotl splayed out flat inside the chamber. "I am quite exhausted, anyway. But know that if I weren't recovering, I would have gladly joined you."

"I'm liking the sound of this new Xotl," Sheni said, beaming. "Hey, how about we all hit the Corpse & Casket after this is wrapped up?"

"That would be lovely. I wonder if I can modify my suit's air filter to include a straw..."

"Get well soon, all right?" Gecki rasped, laying a set of tender claws on the chamber's lid.

Sheni and Alan filed out of the treatment room. Gecki paused in the doorway.

"Not that there's any rush," she snarled wickedly. "I already know I can fly the *Silver Hart* just fine without you now."

"That's hurtful, Gecki."

"Lighten up, you daft starfish," she said with a wink. "In the absence of a backbone, I thought you'd have thicker skin."

CHAPTER
TWENTY-THREE

The auction was held a couple of districts north of Daxos, the area of Kapamentis in which the Ministerium headquarters was based. Sheni, Gecki and Alan took a public transit shuttle over and arrived in a world full of top-of-the-line speeders and two-kilometre tall towers of glass. They presented their identification to the venue's doorman and were ushered into an elevator of emerald and gold.

"I don't think I've ever felt this out of place in my life," Sheni whispered to Gecki once they were up on the eighty-sixth floor. "And I'm counting the time I was caught hiding in the Ark ship's waste recycler."

Normally there'd be no chance Sheni could attend such a fabulous gala. The marble floor was so polished he could see up his own reflection's nostrils. The sections of walls and pillars not draped with opulent banners were even more ornately carved than the archways of Bokata's burial temple. He thought classical Oortilian music was being piped into the chamber until he spotted a trio of blue musicians playing crystalline instruments in the corner. The guests wore corpo suits and glorious robes and sweeping ceremonial gowns while he was kitted out in a spacer jacket and scuffed-up cargo trousers. But as somebody with an item listed in the catalogue, he and his crewmates were automatically entitled to tickets. Not the best seats, mind. They'd be sitting as far back as physically possible. But at least the sparkly drinks were free.

"We ain't the only odd ones out," Gecki rasped as they left the glittery bar. "Look over there, by the twisty plants. Guy looks like he's led a private militia or two in his time."

Trying to render himself invisible amongst the genetically-engineered foliage was a flat-faced, grey-scaled humanoid whose right arm was a high-tech metal prosthesis from the elbow down. In lieu of formal dress he wore a tight-fitting set of black, sleeveless body armour. He noticed them watching him and lifted his bottle of Luethian whiskey in salute.

"I'm pretty sure one of his hands is a literal cannon," Sheni mumbled as he raised a glass and nodded back. "But I suppose if all these swanky socialites and CEOs want the rarest art and artefacts, they've got to rub shoulders with us undesirables at some point."

"Don't assume he ain't just as rich as everyone else. Sell enough relics to wealthy nobs like this lot and pretty soon you're the one with credits lining your pockets. Or maybe he's not selling. Maybe he's loaded coz he raided some Drygg oligarch's mining rig once. Who knows?"

"Yeah, well." Sheni downed his drink and went back for another. "I'm just glad they didn't stick us out back with the wait staff."

Sheni and Gecki kept to themselves and watched the various species intermingle in a perfect storm of faux friendliness and rolling-in-it rivalry. Alan stood on a table, smiling to himself and occasionally sipping from the kwagua juice beside him. The octopod bartender had given him a curly straw long enough to stretch to Barataria and back. Sheni reckoned half the guests had dismissed the small green oddity as a barely animatronic table ornament to complement the lavish flower arrangements.

"It's a shame Xotl isn't well enough to join us," Sheni said with a sigh. "This would be one hell of a first official outing. Just a tad fancier than the Corpse & Casket, that's for sure..."

"Pah, who wants fancy? Xotl just cares about being near their friends. And the atmosphere in the Corpse is way better. This place... it's too delicate. Say the wrong word and your net worth drops by half."

"Won't fall very far for us, then..."

"Esteemed guests," said a loud, deep voice through concealed speakers. "The auction is about to begin. Please make your way to your allocated seats."

"Ooo, here we go." Sheni shivered with excitement as the wealthy patrons filed out of the bar and into the adjacent hall. "It's all very exciting, isn't it?"

"If you say so," Gecki snarled. "Watching a bunch of rich toffs bid on junk they don't need isn't exactly my idea of a good time. I'd rather just skip to the sword."

"Yes, well, I'm sure all the sellers think that." Sheni plucked their crewmate off the table. "Come on, Alan. You can bring your drink so long as you don't spill it."

They joined the back of the crowd and shuffled around the exterior of the auction chamber until they found their designated booth. Even right at the back of the hall, it wasn't shabby, though it was a little cramped for three people. Well, two people and a beachball. The seats were upholstered with red velvet. Installed on the balcony of their booth was a small terminal currently displaying the logo of the auction house.

A feathery waitress paused in the doorway of their booth as they were getting seated and offered them canapés from a silver platter.

"Bivalve carpaccio, sir? Ma'am?"

"Oh, don't mind if I do," Gecki rasped, taking the whole tray. The waitress opened her beak to protest, then headed back to the kitchen in search of more supplies instead.

Sheni popped one of the entrées in his mouth and immediately winced. Yep, definitely raw. The way the mussel meat flapped about on his tongue, he wasn't altogether sure it was dead, either...

"How much do you think it'll go for?" he asked, swallowing it down whole. "The sword, I mean. I know I've been throwing around the millionaire stuff, but..."

"Nah." Gecki sniffed and shook her head. "Not that high. Ignore all that fungus nonsense and all you've got is a rusty old stick. Some weird collector will want it, though. Half a million credits at most, I reckon. Still," she added, nudging Sheni affectionately, "that'll be our biggest haul yet. And this time we get to keep it. *All* of it. You did good, human."

"You wait long enough," Sheni said with a wink, "and stuff always turns up roses in the end."

"Yeah, unless you get killed along the way. But for once it seems your quenchless optimism has actually paid off. Let's put a pin in the celebrations until we actually get paid though, yeah?"

"Hey. We're out of prison, Xotl's on the mend, and the sword's gonna sell for *something*." He raised his glass in a toast. "I figure that's reason enough to celebrate, right?"

Gecki snorted in amusement and reluctantly clinked her glass against his.

"Sure. Whatever you say, ya sappy idiot."

She turned back to the silver tray. All of the sliced mussels were gone.

Alan burped and giggled to himself.

"Oh, quiet, quiet," Sheni said, shaking Alan and shushing Gecki as the lights dimmed. "They're starting."

Gecki rolled her eye, rested her head in her hand, and sighed.

"This is gonna be a long night..."

They watched as tens of millions of credits were spent on relic after relic. The only known portrait of a Jakkashi high-born. A stony section of a cave painting pilfered from an ancient Mansa temple. The preserved head of a rose that blooms only once per hundred years. Eventually Gecki fell asleep out of sheer boredom. But then suddenly Sheni was poking her awake. She closed her drooling jaw with a loud snap.

"We're next," he said excitedly. "Look, there it is."

A glass display case rose from within the floor of the stage. Inside was the rusty old sword, shimmering a sickly green. Sheni hoped the assistants didn't cut themselves getting it ready for the presentation.

"Item number thirty-six," announced the virtual auctioneer, "the legendary Sword of Bokata. Bidding begins at eighty thousand credits."

Alan cooed at the sword in awe and waddled over to the bidding terminal with dollar signs in his bulbous eyes.

"Nope, not this one," Sheni said, pulling him away. "That one's ours, buddy."

He waited for the bids to start flooding in with his heart

sitting in his throat. It wasn't possible to see into any of the booths except for those far on the other side of the auditorium, but attendees could watch the bids roll in via the monitor in their booth's terminal. Some of the previous items had climbed to astronomical figures. Sheni couldn't wait to see what heights a near-mythical sword could reach.

But ten seconds passed without a bid. Then twenty, then thirty. Sheni's heart sank back down, past his chest and into his stomach. Somebody should have bid *something* by now.

"Nothing?" asked the virtual auctioneer. "This is the real sword belonging to the ancient warrior, Bokata. I know you've heard the bedtime stories. Remember, the opening bid need only be a mere *eighty thousand* credits…"

"Nah, you've got to be kidding me." Sheni leaned forward over the balcony. "Bokata's burial temple, Port Providence, Warden Hills's prison – we can't have gone through all that for nothing."

Gecki growled deep in her throat. Gods, he was gonna get an earful about this when they got back to the ship. It hadn't exactly been cheap to list the sword here in the first place…

"Maybe we should have set the starting bid lower," she snarled, baring her teeth at him. "You know, like two hundred credits, or something. You did get it authenticated, right? We didn't put forward some random old pirate's dagger, did we?"

"No, it's the real deal," Sheni whispered back. "Even the Ministry was convinced. But maybe no-one here can bring themselves to believe it…"

A chime rang through their booth. The asking price turned green on everyone's screens.

"And the first bid is in," the auctioneer proclaimed with

gusto. "Eighty thousand credits. Can I expect a counter-offer of one hundred thousand?"

"Hey, that's something, right?" Sheni nudged Gecki. "Enough to keep us fed and the ship in one piece for the next few cycles, for sure!"

The terminal flashed with a new figure just as Gecki opened her mouth to reply. One hundred thousand credits. But before Sheni could perform so much as a fist-pump in celebration, somebody had upped the offer further. And further. And further again. Suddenly the assorted investors and collectors were caught in a frenzy, slashing apart each others' bids almost as quickly as they came in.

"I know my vision ain't always as good as it used to be," Gecki rasped cautiously, "but are you seeing the same numbers I am?"

Sheni said nothing, just nodded. Somebody had poured concrete around his brain and it was setting fast. He could see the number climbing but his mind couldn't keep up with the digits. It certainly didn't believe them. He had to count each of the zeroes twice to be sure.

A countdown timer appeared on the screen of their booth's bidding terminal.

Going once, going twice...

"Sold," the announcer declared, "for twelve point four million credits."

Sheni and Gecki stared blankly as the display case housing the sword descended back into the stage so it could be prepared for the next item. Alan blinked twice and giggled.

"I'm sorry, what?" Sheni mumbled.

Gecki broke into reptilian laughter, a sharp hacking sound that escalated until she was writhing near-hysterically in her seat.

"We're absolutely loaded," Sheni said quietly. His face felt numb. "Filthy rich. No more stealing stuff, no more trawling bars and bandit camps for the next big score..."

Gecki wiped away a tear from her eye with a claw. Sheni turned to stare at her in disbelief.

"What in the galaxy are we supposed to do now?"

THANK YOU FOR READING!

The adventure continues in Shadows in the Sands.

And you might want to check out The Final Dawn if you haven't already – it's the series in which Sheni and the crew of the *Silver Hart* made their first ever appearance.

Turn the page for a full list of titles set in the same universe as Shadows in the Stone.

BOOKS IN THE "DARK STAR PANORAMA" UNIVERSE

Final Dawn Series

- The Final Dawn
- Thief of Stars
- A Dark Horizon
- The New World
- The Tin Soldiers
- Ghost of the Father
- The Stellar Abyss
- The Edge of Night
- The Fatal Dark

War for New Terra Series

- Sigma
- Iron Nest
- Royal Blood

Shadows in the Stars Series

- Shadows in the Stars
- Shadows in the Snow
- Shadows in the Stone
- Shadows in the Sands

Kapamentis Crime Series

- A Cut Below
- Cut to the Bone

- Cut and Shut
- The Final Cut

Standalone Novels

- Saturnalia

SELECT NON-DSP TITLES

- Checking Out (Box Set)
- Blackwater (Box Set)
- The Portrait Lingers Like a Whisper
- Gerald Oddman

WANT A FREE, EXCLUSIVE BOOK?

Building a relationship with my readers is one of the best things about writing. Every now and then I send out newsletters with details on new releases, special offers and other bits of news relating to my books.

And if you sign up to the mailing list I'll even send you a **FREE** copy of *The Ultimate Dark Star Panorama Compendium*, an exclusive guide covering every aspect of my Dark Star Panorama universe, from a full timeline to a comprehensive encyclopaedia. It also contains *Before the Dawn*, a short prequel to my *Final Dawn* series.

Sign up today at twmashford.com.

ENJOY THIS BOOK? YOU CAN MAKE A BIG DIFFERENCE.

Reviews are the most powerful tool in my arsenal when it comes to getting attention for my books. As an indie author, I don't have quite the same financial muscle as a New York publisher. But what I *do* have is something even more effective:

A committed and loyal bunch of readers.

Honest reviews of my books help bring them to the attention of other readers.

If you've enjoyed this book I would be very grateful if you could spend just five minutes leaving a review (it can be as short as you like) on the book's Amazon page.

Thank you very much.

ABOUT THE AUTHOR

Tom Ashford lives just outside London, England with his wife Jenny and extremely needy cat, Kathleen.

An avid movie buff and video game addict, Tom loves all things science fiction. That's why he started the *Dark Star Panorama* universe – an ever-growing tapestry of epic space-faring stories including the *Final Dawn, Kapamentis Crime* and *War for New Terra* series.

His favourite authors are Terry Pratchett and Stephen King.

 facebook.com/TWMAshford
instagram.com/ashfordtom